pot-centric
presented as a rambling narrative

STONER
with a boner

(IT'S A LONG STORY)

A bedside reader for the adult mind

Kathleen K.

For Green Theory
Kathleen K.

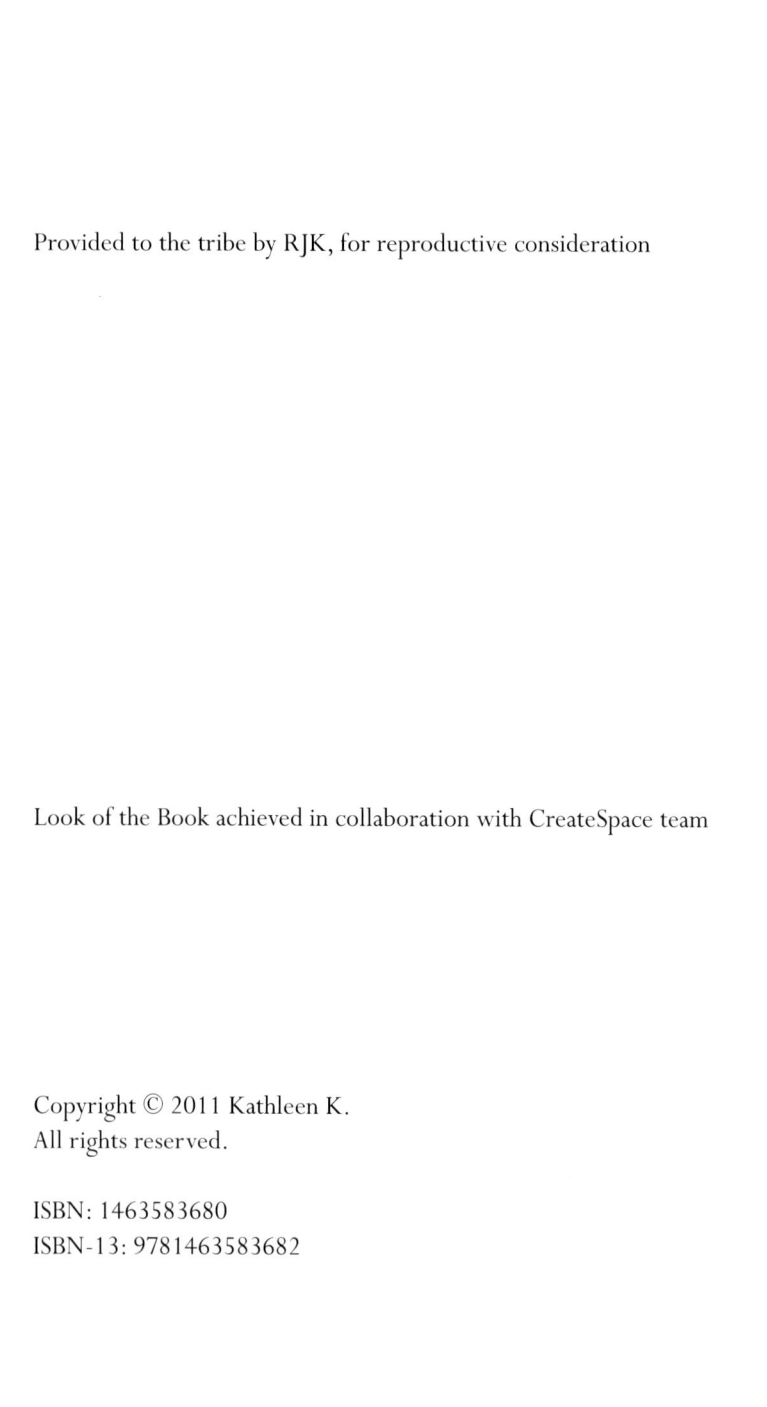

Provided to the tribe by RJK, for reproductive consideration

Look of the Book achieved in collaboration with CreateSpace team

Copyright © 2011 Kathleen K.
All rights reserved.

ISBN: 1463583680
ISBN-13: 9781463583682

if you, like me, like sex and,

like me, like drugs,

you may like sex on drugs, like me

or you might not. and that's cool too.

Stoner with a boner . . . it's a long story. Who knew that I'd look back over so many years when I had been simply living each day, hoping to find something useful to do, something enriching during the day to fund my easy-breezy nightlife – only to notice I had a pot-stained ceiling and bleached-out sheets. And a positive bank balance. (Surprise!)

"This shit tastes sweet."
"Cognac in the bong."

Good sheets washed frequently become a kind of nest; I changed the bed each time I was in it, for sleep or otherwise (especially the otherwise). I wanted to slip into clean sheets every time I approached my bed. This was obsessive but it was attainable. Combinations of a half-dozen bottom sheets and four quilts... mix and match for the weather... snap on the fitted sheet, settle the quilt, toss the pillows. Do it every day and you get faster at it. A few minutes of ritual for the nude nakedness a clean bed invites when it was next peeled open. Never a moment's hesitation at the bedside: Dive! Dive!

"I can't believe you just asked if you could do that to me. Again. How high are you?"
"High enough to keep hoping."

My age-mates and I benefited from the revolutionary 60's when we found ourselves pounding through the rebellious 70's with new presumptions of participation for more people. Social churning resulted in an itch and that itch could be scratched. Drugs in the outlying towns like mine were still mostly weed, speed pretending all sorts of things, an ingredient not the product.... not yet cocaine (powder or rock), not yet heroin (white or brown) – those were deep city drugs, not on the same circuit, juice from a different source oscillating distinctly. We were on campuses and in group houses at the edges of small towns in empty states, working in bead shops and poetry bars, we were young.

We were so healthy that our kidneys and livers could process the toxins and release the feelings, we soared down the highway in our vans, we slept on friends' couches, we ate with strangers, we fucked in the name of peace.

We had no idea that the big, bad 80's would swing our taste for joy to a greed for sensation: more money, harsher highs, until it became deadly to make truly intimate contact.

"That girl you're staring at, I know her name."

"Who are you?" I was looking at one of the many many Joplin-ettes, heavily bangled, her solid stance pugnacious like Janis but lacking (of course) that extra wattage of personal power.

"You don't care who I am. Look, see, she's with a guy I want to talk to so if I could get her to move off him, then I'd have my chance."

"The girl in the white halter?"

"LaLinda. Dig it, LaLinda...The Beautiful."

It was intensely practical for LaLinda and me to keep separate stashes, we each had always had our own way of acquiring and retaining various combustibles and ingestables. We didn't see what that would have to do with whose head was on the neighboring pillow since our drug rituals were personal choices deeply ingrained. I like the taste of unfamiliar bud, it starts at the tip of the tongue then up from the throat to the brain, new combinations were used to keep us floating high. She had some hash, I broke out the opium; she had high octaine ganga, I scraped off two servings of the better opium. Sharing was part of the relationship, I'd met a toker-woman, a rarer bird than the toker-male. LaLinda, not only beautiful but a weed-eater.

Outwardly directed smokers: if with smokers around smoke, they smoke. Inwardly directed smokers: get smoke to take home. Don't kid yourself that there aren't potheads out there, as addicted as anyone who habituates to a stimulation of some sort. As a group, stoners are turned on but at low flame... not looking for a flare-up. They hang back not push forward. Alcohol obliterates thinking in an entirely different way.

↗ ⬇ ↘

Six of us on a crackling dry lawn under the blaze of a noon sun, sensing the sweat bead on our faces. Three couples loosely bound by the hot summer and a shared house, our three apartments conjoining us at the hall, leading us to discover our mutual love of the weed and the intolerable built-up heat a black-roofed red brick building gathers within itself when the city simmers.

Arranged in a curved row on the lawn, apartment A then apartment C and finally my own apartment B with me on the farthest edge, the garden hose looped in my hand, pinched shut then released which started the sprinkler again.

"With this water, I thee wet."

From our toes to our shins, knees, thighs, various pubic arrangements, navels, midriffs, chests/breasts, nipples (nipples!), our upstretched arms, faces, all of us sprinkled with the cool dusting of new drops, not enough to call us drenched but already all our stonedness had gathered and gained in the focus. The sprinkler not at our feet: that would be too close, it was set several yards beyond us so the water reached us evenly from toe to tip as we fanned out from our shared base in half a pinwheel.

How was it LaLinda and I became the leaders? We were not sure when it happened (she didn't even really live there). Our ideas held sway, maybe we were just less spaced than the others who, if not led, tended to slow to stasis.

↗ ⬇ ↘

Road trip. We had a cigar box with papers, scissors, joint stones (to avoid lipping the paper end, a round stone with an air passage through the center held the burning joint at the far end back when joints were <u>big</u>), roach clips ranging from the standby alligator clip to fancy beaded feather clips right up to our prized hemostats – we gathered up anything flat enough to fit inside when the box was hooked shut.

We carried a small valise for the larger items: the seeder tray which allowed the grass to sift through. It trapped the dozens of seeds culled from a rolling session (old days). We always kept seeds around, some germinating in windowsill paddies, others wet in special jars. Sprinkled throughout any government forest in which we hiked, strewn out the car windows on country drives…. We also toked through "shooters", which look like a pliant plastic water bottle, a joint is installed with the lit end inside and the air is shot back out through the joint in a thick stream for the waiting inhalee(s). It is the powerful legacy of the original shotgun, when a joint would be placed ember-side-in between the pursed lips of the smoker who would force a hit back through to the waiting lips of another person: tête-à-tête (one head to another). Very stoner. (Bonus: with a shooter you could fly solo.)

Our destination was a farm about a hundred miles south. We were invited to a large party, the kind you hear about at another party and you know, if you bring beer and snacks, you'll be allowed in but if you bring some grass then you are welcomed.

↗ ⬇ ↘

"Did you say ten grams for a dollar?"
"Don't you wish. Ten bucks for a g."
"How much can I get for twenty-five?"
"Are you messing with me?"

↗ ⬇ ↘

Smoking pot I'd never know the origin of, it comes by in pipes, on clips; the lovely LaLinda has gathered a small crowd around her hand-colored joints, she does this so she can follow her stuff through the crowd, it is appreciated for what it is: the work of artistry. [Not having any idea we had only the roughest materials with which to work, the simple sativa, our marijuanistry may have been crude. Indica awaited.[1] (Differences in the terpenoid content of the essential oil may account for some of these differences in effect.) We loved our dope nonetheless, naughty but nice vice.]

There are people who intrigue me at this party, it is large enough that all of us feel it is possible there might be one other person of truly suitable type— if only we could find them among the attendees, the drunk dancers, the straights sniping in the corner, and the tripping star gazers. We wanted to meet stoners like ourselves, people who would walk to a field and dance, people who knew what it meant to lay down on a roof and let the dark-moon-stars and the earth-water-wind have you.

Possibilities were the coins of my generation, we would talk of life and death with the buzzed and unbuzzed and diff-buzzed. There was a beer marathon on the front lawn; whiskey drinkers slouched on the back porch. Stoners might be in the basement, or the upstairs hall… not right at the front door. Circumstantial smokers might join us but drop out when the green got dark and had accumulated in the group.

Eyelids not fully lifted, pupils open wide yet abstruse, recondite, not merely dark but textured, some of it inward, some outward, how often did our visions slide together, what was and what wasn't, the blurring between thoughts, paranoia a sort of anticipation: this is the bad which *could* happen, it could even if it hadn't, yet (had it?).

I still see LaLinda flashing her collar bones, her dear feet shod in something perfect: cowboy boots at a barn party, brogans on our hill climb, sandals for the beach. With her as my companion, our evenings were at least going to generate enough interest in her exterior to chance a gander back at the gazer's agenda. I'd watch people watch her.

We wanted to dissolve somewhere, a place where the joints might reorganize our molecules (where you were beyond thought and didn't need to be monitoring your brain to operate your heart and lungs). We would be on a waterbed in candle gleam, or in somebody's pool with the underwater lights on… our bodies in the glory of youth presentable in any garb, chasing off stragglers in terry cloth robes, trading shooters in a speedo and clogs… we were busy as could be and excruciatingly casual.

"LaLinda, I swear— I thought it was cool."

"Narcs! There were fucking bloody bloody fucking narcs there."

"Well, they have to be somewhere, unless we've all just imagined them. It stands to reason they'd be where we went to buy drugs, if you think about it "

" I don't want to think about it. You go play with the narcs, I can't afford to be trapped in that reality."

"LaLinda, please, it's over. We saw them and we passed on by."

"Once again, only luck to prevent absolute disaster."

"Too many people heard about the stash, that's why the narcs showed up. You gotta have some discretion with Lucy in the Sky. You don't tell

Kathleen K.

strangers you're dealing sheets of dreams… the hippies stampede like brokers on a hot stock."

"You're tripping."

"Yes, I am. And you're not helping."

↗ ⬇ ↘

Girls, chicks, sisters, women, people… metamorphosis in language ∴ ⚡ ∴ perception. Silly passions of the early teens, my straight sober virgin self, encased in a hard shell of shyness and manners, careful to edge around the perimeter. Back when I was a boy and I all I wanted was a girl to walk with me and talk to me, to go steady and make out and VALIDATE me. Without a girl to distinguish me from the other hopeless hopefuls, I could not imagine how I'd break free from my adolescent egg.

Ursula (not her real name) was smarter than me in math, science and history but I was blessed with a backyard swimming pool. I gathered up a renegade gang of kids who didn't have pools but had assets I lacked (one, a car; another, fake ID "just in case") and by the end of junior year in high school, Ursula was my girlfriend. She contributed class to our group. She and I used to kiss and rub our outfits against each other, nothing more than that; our intimacy (in my mind) came from holding hands at church or presuming you'd have company to attend a school event (football game, search and rescue volunteers, whatever… together). To be publicly linked with Ursula was to have a place. I saw myself in favorable juxtaposition to my girlfriend.

Kelley had no idea Ursula existed when she happened to notice me on a school yard bench. I was alone (no rarity) waiting for some kids to set up the school trampoline when Kelley bounced up to me and asked me to watch her stuff while she tumbled. After an impressive series of rolls, twists, flips, splits and walk-overs, Kelley came to rest at my feet in a victory arch that made my testicles pop. I didn't dare speak but was relieved to notice her belongings hadn't been stolen while I stared open-mouthed at her limber display. Kelley forever-after performed in my fantasies, it was the simple beauty of imagining nude gymnastics. Ursula's fantasy magic was rubbed out by the kinetic rightness of Kelley's position in space. Kelley used energy to satisfy her need to be in motion. She gulped air to power herself, she practiced to be better.

Ursula was still my girl when I was being a boy. Kelley put tang in my romantic fantasies and brought them closer to the sharpness necessary in adult relationships; oh, how I yearned to tell Kelley what I felt but I was afraid it would ruin her easy, friendly acceptance of me as a buddy – from which intimate vantage I gathered up the stupendeous details of her astounding body. For me, for years, merely imagining somebody's private parts in as much detail as I could extrapolate would turn out to be absolutely satisfying. It was obvious in those teen-age pairings of action and imagination that we were interlocking and still discrete, still separable. [Over the years, I'd had light brushes with deeper feelings but not until LaLinda did I put my love and sex worlds together.] Back then I suspect Kelly knew I wanted her that other way, she didn't mind that as long as I didn't make a move on her, and I was fine with it. I didn't want to be expected to move. I wasn't ready. I was thinking thinking thinking about it.

✍ ⬇ ↘

Started smoking grass right after I met Kelley, a pure coincidence in timing. My cousin from Ohio brought some along to the family reunion and we toked it after the adults were smashed on bourbon and beer. I felt a beckoning freedom, I slid into a mind-set and REGISTERED on the world. I'm not sure I would have trusted anyone else from my daily life, like a school mate, but sneaking off with a cousin while still proximate to family made my first high very low risk. I wouldn't do it again for six months after that, the first time stained me deeply with some incredible knowledge: lawbreaking (!) could go undetected. It was harmless, naughty, and I was wised up to the essential conflict of not only knowing the rules but applying them to actual life.

Kathleen K.

Marijuana is an expansive drug, it made me want to lift my arms and gesture with open hands, I liked the idea of leaning forward but spared the energy and didn't. Inside myself I felt the wiggle of my center, I was not screwed on tightly but my threads were straight. In that silken seam existed a languor in which I could connect with a woman, a chick, a girl like the often-imagined Kelley. She would let me fire the end of my doobie, and suck through a couple major hits. Her contact high would not be fake, she would dreamily remove her sweater and skirt, revealing plain underwear on the nubile body of an innocent virgin. She would do a back bend, making me reach forward.

Grass now lets me blend my fantasies and realities into a livable life, it was hard for me to make peace juggling the day-to-day of staying alive with the loose roaming customs of my tribal group, the pot-head stoners... I want to emphasize that these are dualities of the same space. Without the convenience of Amsterdam hash bars, I had to flit around neighborhood taverns to find the marijuana nomads. In later years when I joined a forming-group of fellow tokers, it wasn't important that I identify myself as a grocery store manager... I was the guy with the good rolling papers. There was nothing to be gained by expanding the surface that I presented to them... there was at-work and there was not-at-work.

The work part of my life was simple because I kept it that way: I worked on the store at the store. I goofed off on my time off. I had simple rules for the employees of the store, me included:

(1) Be there.
(2) Work.
(3) Get paid.

I stressed a clean store and quick check-outs which pleases the customers. There was no need for fancy management theories and lots of staff meetings. You kept moving the whole time you were on the clock, you took your breaks on schedule, lunch ditto then, back to work until quitting time. There was plenty to do and I made sure it got done quickly and well. It was "bread and butter" work providing food for families, couples, and singles; we could understand the quality control issues, we knew our customers, we consumed our own merchandise.

It was easy to arrange things to suit me. Most grocery managers feel compelled to supervise the delivery of goods. I prefer to negotiate the supply <u>and</u> delivery standards at mid-day mid-week meetings with sales reps. I was a good payer and didn't make it difficult to please me: get what I order to the store and I'll sell it to pay my bills. End of story. I came in latest on Tuesday, after lunch; Wednesday and Thursday in at noon, Friday my "early" day at ten and Saturday at three so I'd be there through to midnight. The assistant managers were left alone to manage mornings and Sunday – it was their time to shine. I might pop in to do my shopping, experiencing the store as a customer who had to push a cart and find the brown sugar. (More often, I trolled the aisles of a competitor, buying sparingly of items we didn't stock, plus a trip to an adjacent pharmacy for condoms and lubes.)

I didn't believe I had to be on site to be an influence on the store; if employees understood our common mission then things went smoothly because, by definition, the merchandising was simple. We kept shelves stocked, prices updated, and the warehouse treated our stockroom like an efficient extension of their own. Vendor reps usually try to boost volume by sweet talking at a store, troubleshooting for the merchandisers higher in the chain. I had no problem getting down to brass tacks with a money-motivated seller and couldn't care less if a vendor didn't want to do business with me. No special fees, no under-the-counter deals.

On the existential level, I was in the market to provision people and was at peace with what I was doing. It was not possible for me to completely forsake the adult world even as I skipped around its wild heart at night.

"We'll split it, 50-50."
"I don't have a scale…"
"One splits it, the other chooses first."
"Diabolical!"

↗ ⇩ ↘

Imagine: closing time at an "80's youth bar" where the owners sold high priced, low quality booze to people who were choosing drinks by the type of glass in which they were served. The almost/just-turned-legal crowd gulped sweet wines, rum and Coke, White Russians, and they toked weed in the parking lot. Non-dancers watched dancers boogie down to mediocre local bands, happy to be pressed together in the small club, guaranteed to feel like part of the crowd. I would see a solo girl guarding a pile of purses at a table and know not only was she "off" in some respect (or she'd be dancing) but also that she had a good car, or her own apartment, and would be using that asset to bind her friends to her. I could see a slutty one and know if she'd do it in the alley or not... most wouldn't but the ones who would, would do so without much fuss, it would be crazy-hot sex quickly finished. Fine by me, as long as she starts it.

Back then I was freshly aware of the gorgeous female form, I was newly acquainted with my voluptuous satin-skinned peers. I was at peak, I see it now, and had glimpses of it even back then, the feeling when I ran for distance or slid myself between smooth soothing thighs to balance on my golden bone. This might be how a new car would feel when it hit cruising speed on the highway.

↗ ⇩ ↘

"This grass is no good."
"It never comes through."
"I don't get off on it, not quite— I'm almost off."
"It would take like, maybe, about sixteen more THC molecules..."
"No, that's not the problem, there's plenty of molecules but they don't add up right, the chemistry is off."
"I could probably trade it back for some mushrooms."
"Liberty Caps aren't in season."

"No, Redboner says he eats these other 'shrooms and then when he's in the woods he can sense the presence of that specific mushroom in his vicinity."

"I hear he finds them growing under cow patties, that's why they taste like shit."

"Are you sure we aren't high?"

"You shouldn't have to ask."

I was so full of crap when I was new to sex. I got the message finally but until then I did think girls were lucky to get a guy's attention. How much more obvious could it have been that mathematically there were a sufficient number of jocks and class presidents and musicians available to the best babes? An ordinary guy like me could expect to connect straighter across the board to someone equally ordinary. Merely shifting my sights to the actual pool from which I would draw gave me an advantage against the other males who couldn't admit they wouldn't get the cheerleaders or valedictorian – they would come late to their actual level. Moving forward quickly gains this particular ordinary male the cream of the ordinary females.

I was once reminded *during the act* that I was "just balling", *nothing serious* because this person had no intention of giving me a kid or anything REAL. Ka-pow. Perfunctory may sound too harsh but if it has a kinder sense then I refer to that same old koo-koo-ka-choo we all know and have a taste for. I had never felt "tolerated" before, borderline "used": I didn't like it.

I was mechanically qualified as a man but judged short on the genetic level, she was looking for taller, leaner, being neither herself.

Kathleen K.

Certain women have a way of pressing forward in their bodies so you know that they are moving closer to you, they can't help it, it is the opposite of shrinking from something repulsive, in each case you feel you are having an impact upon them.

An opposite image, of the man coiling inside, has to do with the gender's habitual chest-out posture. Analysis: if that manly chest is carried up-and-out and still astoundingly he has reserve— he can more than roar!!

Mom and the father were well-matched before they made me, they wrote songs together and basically were beatniks with jobs at a song factory. It is no wonder I'm the way I am, it's running in the family. My mother still speaks of "the father" as if her life was a stage play and his role off-tangent, sufficient to describe him as a noun rather than an individual man. I was the audience. Whether he left her (us) or she (we) left him is not explicit: they split. Period. I went with "the mother" but I was allowed to call her Mom (that would be in character, you see?). Swirl them together and you get a me.

When it comes to love I first need to get past my handsome face.

An ordinary face would not go with this dapper body, this body which is not dainty only because I bulk up to prevent that very fate. I fight against the fact I'm slight in build by thickening it with muscle. My bones are springy and perfect for running in the woods, dashing away from larger predatory creatures. Within my species, I have a face which traditionally means, "trust me, don't step away, let me hold your attention". Etched in the angles of my brow and jaw, the definition of my lips against the texture of my skin— the geometric balance that even babies recognize is a good combination. You must understand I'd be different if I looked differently. (So would you.)

It is what it is, not what it was, not what it ought to be, not what it might be. It is what it is – until it isn't.

Benign criminals confuse the law abiding folk, how can misbehavior not be antisocial? In fact, for criminals like me involved with the pot underground, we specifically avoid harming ourselves or others because being stoned is a delicate balance easily lost in confrontation. I know that the "big business" end of marijuana is probably as scary as the worst labor union, as twisted as the corrupt enforcement organizations set to police them. That is one of the reasons I do smoke, because the human race has a nature that tends to blur the facts of their existence; I'm looking for redirection, smoke swirls through me, spinning me ahead.

We prefer to turn from the kind of facts that tell us people least able to support the burden of children reproduce in the largest numbers – we set that aside. Paving over the planet isn't a good idea yet we keep the mixers turning, turning. Nature balanced the competing needs of countless species, but she may have been goosed by man – it would be just like us! We will kill the bees that carry the pollen to fertilize flowers for birds who feed mammals from whose skin we make coats and boots… life without leather? Meat? Grain? Air?

I'm "green" meaning I'm earth-oriented and planet-proud; I think we should fill our days celebrating the wonder of life and toward that end I fight the everyday society with an agenda of my own. Cultivating a secret plant of dream weed from fortified soil with the help of a sun collector teaches me the life of the plant, from its hopeful first shoot to its dark resin. This reassures me I am simply harvesting a bounty of nature. I do not need to assemble a chemistry lab. One potted pot plant. Grow, cut, dry, bake or burn (ingest or inhale).

Some party pot makes you over-sensitive to reality and the resultant haze makes you disbelieve what you observe, this can be a problem if you attempt to communicate to the non-high and the differently-high. This is interpersonal danger, your cool is being tested. Keep attention to the present time. Connect with your companion by asking to walk with them out the door, volunteer to be cut away from the main herd, avoid being branded. There is a chemical reaction to the ingredients of this spectacular plant and that is its magic, its beauty, and a measure of my own control that I stand back even as I am drawn into it. Feel what you feel instead of observing and commenting upon it, forget yourself and let the world work around you.

Sex while stoned, not quite the same dispassion as a just-friends high because the intoxication involves more than just the brain... the body is beyond belief.

I kept wondering if I was over-acting on my fucking orgasms; whack jobs resulted in the same pounding heart and tensing thighs, the corkscrewed desire heating inside me, but I did not cry out, did not clutch the sheets in the same way I pressed my partner to me at the extreme moments of our sex together. I got off on the stereophonic nature of vocalizing with my partner because I felt strangled when I held back my pleasurable growls and praise to God (damn, that's fine).

I was taught to consider my partner in all my social actions: female relatives made it plain they were participating in the world in a way their own mothers had abdicated. Even when looking for the naughtiest girls, I found the self-sufficient ones. I was not fooled into thinking that my immature selfish antics were more important than they were, and never (ever) was it casual to throw a kid into somebody. I never thought to put that burden on any of my partners. It was great if she joined in the contraception but in all cases I did *everything* I could to avoid pregnancy short of The Snip.

My uncle spoke to me of marriage, in place of my absent dad, describing the state of grace within a family, of loyalty as a virtue and commitment its manifestation. Before being capable of accepting that level of involvement, wild behavior had life and death at its root. Do not mistake the joyride as a means of transportation, it is stupidity for the sake of metamorphosis – you change with each risk – you age with every mile, even happy laughs foster wrinkles. Also, he made me understand, when the golden age of wild oats came upon a person, it was a duty and an honor to sow them with personal style. To scatter them, all of them, then.

↗ ⬇ ↘

She was wrapped in clothes. A turban she unrolled first, letting down a tangle of orange-tipped brunette hair. A scarf unwound from her tanned throat, a cape around her freckled shoulders…. a silver tube top (in this weather!) above a wrap-around skirt made of red velvet… slave slippers with the long laces twining around her ankles, calves, shins. My darling beauty contained away from the dirty world, the world full of callous youths like me who would make love to a woman I didn't understand for reasons I couldn't specify. She must have had a few loose thoughts of her own because she engaged this callous youth (at her age!).

Arlene stripped for me, it was a process that did not require my assistance but benefited from my attendance. I didn't have to wonder what she saw in me, I was pure raw rarely-touched manhood and I knew that was my prime value. I was protected from knowing how much more there was to it because, frankly, I barely could control the callous thoughtless relations. How would I have dared to actually communicate with a woman who knew to dress like that for me? It helped that I was selfless at times like that, intruding with personal insights would have stalled the woman for whom I played puppet. Toy with the puppet, fuck with the puppet, forget the puppet… happy puppet. And, remember, there are other puppets and other women who like puppets.

I didn't judge the reasons a woman got naked with me, I tried to present my best credentials, never knew which key worked on the opening for speech, for touch, for blending. I was hopeful, I was healthy, I offered myself to women far distanced from my peer group. Why not? My oats sought foreign pastures but still I hunted the open gate.

I dreamt I was the head guy running a lingerie factory – it would be clean and bright, full of work islands where purposeful people cooperated to frame the breast, belly, bottom. We would flatter the style of one woman at a time. Panties, boxers, swim cut, thigh-hi, bikini, hi-kini, thong. How many curves need to be added to encircle the carnal globe? How can you fault the theory of evolution if it carved Audrey Hepburn out of the simian Lucy or Tina Turner from the mythic Eve. How much more mysterious that these characteristics spruce up a guy like Lucky Vanous – to look touchable and edible and likable to many many who see you. Borderline too good to be true. That gives them a confidence as individuals to appear as symbols (models).

I would talk to the panty designers about maintaining lift, achieving separation, affecting buoyancy. The fabric department would share samples, explain why this lace would not suit the junior line; I'd invent a slippery non-snag fabric for the sake of the working man's hands. Always I'd be asking, Does this please you? Is this right? Should we make more like this? Tell me how it feels. Tell me how it makes you feel.

Yes, I love to bury my cock in the liquid-lined crease of flesh, gateway to the foyer of life, the vestibule, the place you make offerings, the site not accessible without cooperation (nullified by force). That first time and its other iterations, the mild fear that this may be the last (and if it is, it must be the best!) (but how to judge: deepest in, longest held, the tight fit or the right fit?). Yieldings as separate sighs and cries, the silent slipping of skin: some of it rubbing together, some of it peeling apart. Slapping and crackling, too lusty for some, so many aspects to keep hidden even if you surrender topical access.

Not all my choices, sometimes I've been stuffed into a waiting hole, the handiest thing of a moment, as if cocks had been lined up on a table and mine selected *to try out*. Sat upon or backed up against, my stick taken into the cooze, my driving power not required (not invited) ((not accepted)) (((not tolerated))).

Nothing better than fucking a fucking woman, women who merely confer access aren't fucking you and you know it, there is no velocity, you can't rev the motor, you may have a marvelous time but you are not fucking.

The verbal use of fucking has been diluted by people (who mustn't actually fuck) using the word improperly. What word will replace it? Is there anything as essentially provocative as a word we kept hidden on our broadcast bands for many decades, the no-no finally blurted on network TV, bleeped but readable on the lips... no wonder we're having saran-wrapped sex, we don't respect the inner-powers that make the scent of a person overcome social considerations and you end up balling your landlady. Hypothetically.

🖎 ⬇ 🖎

Through it all, the casual access to quality bud. We were a stoner community, always with reefer on hand. Not living off the smuggling money, none of us did more than deal for our own stash, we were part of the underground railroad of herbalists. There were lean times, we had outages, but they were noticed, they were CURED and we got back in the groove we preferred, the mist of consensual reality-blurring where we cooperated to be happy individuals.

Some friends and I lucked into two income sources: we put together intricate puzzles and framed them for sale. Our trademark was to leave the edge pieces off, as if the puzzle might go on and on in all directions, sculpted not squared. We also made hooked yarn rugs. We'd buy rolls of interlock rug canvas and the artistic among us would color designs to be filled in by who ever could figure out how to use a latch hook. We had set up four rug tables, and two puzzle tables, in the living-dining room of a communal house. There were pocket doors that were pulled closed to keep the air fresh, you could *be* high but you could not *get* high in there. Friends were welcome, and hours would go by as people came, helped, left... it was collegial, we listened to comedy albums and FM radio.

Later, the pot community would seem to shrink but there were enough of us left to create a social ripple, we were the voice towards de-criminalization of marijuana, more like 3.2 beer with government-imposed age and activity limits. A venial sin, a misdemeanor, it could compound criminal charges (stoned robbery, stoned hit and run, etc., would be punished more severely). In time we were joined by the medical community who found marijuana's stomach-calming properties *perceived by the users* to be superior to any chemical substitute *which contributed to its efficacy*. For their patients who were being beaten up by cancer therapies, somehow *they were convinced* getting high cut through the nausea which let them eat which helped them live. As the age in government shifts upward, our candidates haul along college backgrounds that could well have included dorm smokers, binge drinking, liberal sex.

Weed is a naturally occurring substance, it should be cultivated for commercial purposes like we do with sugar or coffee, provided in the market place like medicine, like wine, like bullets. Let's stop the cat and mouse on weed, save that enforcement budget for the speed labs and crack houses where the gap is clearly visible between tolerable and intolerable. I have established a quiet room with wood shutters on both windows, a mat unrolls to seal the door, there are shaded lamps, it is not dark-themed, more like sand colors, sea grasses, clouded skies. I listen to music, to the surge of my emotions, I want to be alive to the extent I am capable. I'm not a major league player in public-approval roulette; I'm out there doing my job and earning my rewards.

Intoxicants should be controlled, pot included, because in fact it really isn't good in large doses, it profits from moderation like all things do; still it gives young adults something to build a rebellion around from which they have a good chance to recover. Most of us slow down when stoned, if not actually stop, *and pot will let you go unlike speed, unlike heroin, unlike cocaine, unlike alcohol.*

The relentless amount of marijuana necessary to become physically wrecked is usually stemmed by becoming mentally wrecked first. You don't get mastermind-type criminal projects accomplished when you're blasted. Not likely to complete a neurosurgery residence toking regularly either. Some things don't mix. Pot can be used to forget to succeed as well as to find a new way to define success.

☝ ⬇ ↖

Together: stoned and screwing. How much more beautiful could life be? I fell into the well of youth and vigor, crawled out each morning and got back to work, forgetting the sight of my new love twirling on a dance floor or advancing naked to my clean-sheeted bedside. Those ideas got racked behind the store's imperative demands because the consumers existed and simply had to be served, I didn't have to wonder at my purpose or my achievements. The store was very very real. On the plus side, when I wasn't at the store I was all the way gone and didn't let it worry me. That's why I had good employees, I let them be busy.

☝ ⬇ ↖

Stupid me, younger me I mean. I was rolling in clover, honey. My body was at its peak of performance, I was in my mid-twenties and everything worked. I am not in bad shape now FOR MY AGE; however, back then, I was in the expected health state: PERFECT. It isn't only me who realizes that youth is wasted on the young. Still, like many intoxicants, the self-pleasure of a young body would probably blow the circuits of a thinking individual. Best to be brainless, to be reactive, to be so self-absorbed as to fail to register the actuality of your condition. If only my rich, mature thoughts had that just-hatched flesh to animate.

LaLinda! Naked she had the shine of a pearl, a luminescent surface serving as boundary for the eyes: do look at the outside, do not peer inside. My glance would slip off the cool smoothness of her exterior, her eyes a window to her soul, yes, all her openings enthralled me because I knew her true beauty was hidden.

By then I had so much experience with casual sex that it was sometimes difficult to have fun. I'd seen so many possibilities that I felt obligated to spin permutations until I found the correct combination, I was thinking too much about what I was doing just so my partner wouldn't think I wasn't thinking. We had fragile connections.

LaLinda made me reduce my agenda to getting next to naked her naked.

Harmonic tremors in the earth, likes vibes between people, think of it!

Dilemma: pick a partner, or be picked. If being picked, I would have to decide if I was bait or catch. Was just my surface attractive (bait) or would I be a quality guy: catch? If a fish was easily tricked by bait, she bit quick. If I was doing the choosing, I'd withstand that first flurry of interest, wait to see who sat further back in the bar, who was too busy to look at me. Those memories are fond, too much alcohol and pot, if you want to be objective, but the glory of unhinged senses is the province of the innocent. Continuity is over-rated for the young, a boon to the aging. The difference is off-road travel in a borrowed car, and interstate traffic in something registered with the government at the place mortgaged in your name.

I made sure to learn first names during serious flirtation, I took the time to get mine across. It seemed ridiculous not to get this simple handle on your partner. It made things very ordinary for a moment, exchanging basic information: your neighborhood (way too soon for an address), your basic situation for the evening (but always say, here with friends).

Helen. Bobbette. Micki. Fleur. Judith. Starr. Su. Cathryn. Somehow I always kept an image of a baby being christened, here begins your life, Rhonda, Ellen, Ann Marie, Rusty, Trixie, Belle. As, in one singular moment, their future like mine became the meanderings of an officially named person. Bronwyn. Pratima. Siobhan.

↗ ⇩ ↘

I remember rolling around more with the ladies. We would fall off beds, although back then we might be tangling on a twin, unlike the roomy bed in which I can now afford to sleep and/or entertain. I lived with rug burns, I would hump across the kitchen floor on a wooden chair, I balled my way up a curving staircase, one fucking step at a time!

Laughing was easy, crying didn't last.

↗ ⇩ ↘

She was an ordinary girl in a wheelchair, back then she'd be carried, wheels and all, over the many barriers in her way – ramps were rare. She was unable to travel alone, even from her front door to the mailbox, so of course over time she didn't get her own mail (the caregiver was going to get the mail in any case, the question became whether she 'needed' to go along). I considered this a significant detail as to the facts of her life.

She was at a party I was at, I realized she was probably stranded in the kitchen due to the simple step up from that room to the living room (heart of the party). We talked for a while, she ate most of a hash brownie before I thought to wonder if she knew it was spiked. Her caretaker had the night off and the substitute thought it would be "therapeutic" to "get out and about". No problem to hoist her up the back steps, back her into a corner. Job done, eh?

That's probably what got me connected to her, I thought the caretaker was doing a shitty bit of work. I could do better, and would do better for free. I spent over an hour in her company, impressed by her appreciation of the party. Still, I didn't know what to say when she commented that the brownies were gritty and bitter... she recognized the odor of pot drifting in the from the living room and didn't ask to indulge. Not to suspect the baked goods of being party-packed with drugs was elementally innocent for which I liked her even more (although I also thought I'd mark the different treats somehow at my next party, flags maybe...). She was about to reach a higher plane. (I was already there.)

I got lost in the thought of how long it had been since I'd had the pleasure to like a female my age without sexual potential (interference). Got jolted out of that thought pattern by a powerful hand on my upper leg. She was saying I looked strong enough to help her escape outside to the sidewalk where at least she could roll away from the people who seemed to be crowding us in the kitchen. She said she'd never been so dreamy which I could understand: hash brownies make you anti-gravitate. No matter which idea flutters near, your mind smoothly spins away from it. She and I st/rolled along outside. I had no reason to de-sex her, no matter how often I was deflected from that familiar speculation (what would we do, how would we do it?). Desire returned in various forms: noticing her smooth shoulders, impressed by her well-behaved hair, amazed at my own selfishness (worse, what was I doing presuming she lacked the ability to "feel" intimacy?).

She said, "I wouldn't go to bed with a guy on the first night no matter what, so you try not to think about that – until later. I'd want to know the guy a whole lot better than I know you at this point. But, I could use some flirting, couldn't you? Straighten a lock of my hair, lift the tip of your index finger to the underpoint of my chin, lick my lips."

"Oh. That's a lot of words to say, good ones though. It's official: I'm stoned. Hash in the baked goods. Did I tell you that?"

"Is that what this is?"

"Sure. Stoned is OK. Those brownies finish baking <u>in</u> your brain. I think it's the calories from the sugar burning extra brightly on your lips."

"Speaking of lips, do you think I don't know you want to kiss me? I'm leaning so far forward I'm afraid the chair's going to spill me out. Would it be too much for you to kneel for me?"

"I would bow to you."

"Except I don't want to kiss the top of your head. You've never had an experience like this, have you?"

"Nope."

"Well, lucky for us, I have. So, I'll be in charge of the boundaries, you move us within them."

↗ ⬇ ↘

Memory stirs memories. Back, deep in time. Remembering her reminded me that kissing LaLinda had evolved into suckling at an atmosphere created between us, as thick as shared hope, pliant with life-giving energy. Nothing compared to the beneficent expanse of our locked lips, eyes darting beneath closed lids, making the mind wipe itself clean, believing that you were soul mates when you could kiss like that.

LaLinda found a way to withstand my first kisses (which later I realized she would have disliked). I thought it was good to grind your faces together. LaLinda needed me to stay back so she could thrust her own lips forward, towards me, intended to dock against my own puckered pout. You lose so much surface in a pout that LaLinda rarely presented pursed lips, more often she'd cover one of your lips with both of hers, kissing in the corners of your mouth.

She spoiled me in some ways for other women because when we were very good together, nobody else could matter.

My to-remain-unnamed lover in the wheelchair had bruised her spine and it never really healed. There was no break in the cord but the signals to her legs came through weakly even with her greatest effort. She could feel deep sensation faintly. She used leg braces and a walker at least three hours a day and had a magnificent upper body. By forcing herself erect she kept her legs and butt aligned.

The splendor of that woman stretched out before me! I turned her on to good pot and she liked it. We'd get ourselves all set up in the boudoir, fire up the bong and floor-dance to the Grateful Dead and ELO. We'd be on our chaise lounges, holding hands and talking stoner talk, discussing nothing thoroughly. I'd admire her and she'd toss off my compliments. We both knew she was hoarding them to savor in private. I wasn't sure how to say that her restricted movement was not important to me except in the real sense of loss I felt for her. She was great fun to be with and rich in erotic experience while I got to play ganga-guide to her.

What could be sweeter than the two of us giggling naked, she was the sort of person who got tough when she was… stimulated. She roughed around with me, she was a fully grown woman, good sized, a haven. I was a naughty boy who slipped in after dark to partake of her abundance. Our age difference was not great but our maturity levels varied. She was a secret resource, I was pulled toward her stark femininity. We would talk about our futures, we both had the hope for love. It was not to be found between us and became a safe topic to explore in rambling conversations.

Memory: The day I realized LaLinda would never ever get married. That was final. A knowing.

↗ ⬇ ↘

It seemed to me that marriage would be, in part, like my day job, a fact of my life, something that I would connect through, a structure for my existence. I am prone to mild vice, I like the little kicks you get from gambling once in a while, tokin' the illegal weed... ohh, wicked me. Otherwise, I considered myself a bargain-keeper and a hard worker. That would count in my favor with a woman seriously seeking a mate like me.

I've thought about it. I think my dad "wasted" my mother in a way, he didn't give her enough credit for her contribution to our family's success. Now he sings her praises to his second wife, having total recall of the very many services provided to him by his never-thanked, uncelebrated, now-piously-mourned first wife. I want to do better than that. I might have been able to do that with LaLinda, if she'd wanted that, but she didn't so we'll never know.

It was, as she said, precluded.

↗ ⬇ ↘

I'd get up early on Saturday mornings, very early, like 5:30, and do some horrible project like wash all my windows (no sun streaking) or clean out the kitchen cabinets. I'd work like hell then take a shower and go back to bed until noon— or even later— secure that I'd already done my project for the house, the rest of the day would be gravy.

I'd put myself in a stoned state of mind, the world quiet with early morning shadows, and attack my project with due diligence. I'd take everything off the walls in the kitchen and scrub them down, touch up the paint at the corners, reduce clutter. I had to do this to survive because my place was small.

Kathleen K.

I liked living alone, I was going to miss that when (if) I got married. You never know about yourself until you are independent and in crisis, lose a job, suffer a loss, an emotional meteor strikes your life. I can remember subsisting on noodle-roni food while I waited for my rental deposit check to clear the bank— I needed a place for me alone and could not risk any delay in getting an anchor point. I'd eat later, in my new place.

My condo may have been built tidy like a ship but the shared facilities made it feel like living in a spa. There was a clean, clear pool, an indoor all-purpose court for basketball or handball or kids tossing baseballs (no windows). The full service laundry ran night and day. I got over my shyness and learned to separate my clothes into the this-is-one-load flat-bottomed bags then deposit them down a hall chute for "processing". There were a thousand ways I'd be more comfortable living here than the house-share I hated, and I knew it, so I plunked every bit of cash I had on the deposit. I was due for a "next level" increase at the food chain, I'd dogged my way up the ladder and here was my reward: a grown-up space all to myself.

⌦ ⇩ ⇘

"How did sand get here on the counter?"
"It's sugar, we're making cookies; we're not at the beach."
"I know that. Please to excuse the brain fart."

I don't know where pot gets its bad reputation as an existential demotivator... I've never had any problem realizing that I had to make something of my life, herb or no. I could never have been a corporate suit, I had to see some tangible value of my effort, and groceries were as real-world as you can get. I got very specific in the interview for store workers: do you wear a watch? You ever clean a toilet – and not just the inside of the bowl, I mean the base and the wallboard behind it? What is the difference between a peach and an apricot (they're cousins in the rose family, as a matter of fact, but an apricot is closer to a plum in the eyes of the shopper.) I watched out for fibbers and the sly.

Successful candidates had filled in their forms neatly and completely, they arrived on time for the interview (wore watches), they were not rude to the service clerk (I always check) and if they didn't know an answer they said so. I didn't cotton to the smarmy ones so mostly my crew members were strong individuals with team-work structure around them. Routine was our watchword. Stuff got clocked in the back door and was tracked on its way through the inventory to the shelf/bin/rack and— hope of all hopes— through the checkout.

I'm gratified at the end of each quarter we complete without an injury accident, without a quality recall, without a robbery.

Hedonism, self-indulgence, enriching the experience of a moment, what's so bad about a little of that? Elusive excitement, the few things that truly trip your trigger, how is it that the brain knows to lower its barriers, to dream, to drive on autopilot, to sleep through sirens and wake at a child's cough... to coordinate a genital climax through the fingertips when so much of it is in your head?

Erotic fulfillment is rare and much appreciated in my life. The few times I hooked up with straight (non-toking) women, I had as good a time as ever. Pot made it different, but sex was plenty good without it. I loved being touched as we prepared for sex, a hand stroking circles on my back or warming my hip. I reacted to a rump rub, I didn't respond to nipple-pinching or licking but a flat hand pressing against my chest wall felt good. I liked to give and get hickeys because while the sucker sucked, the suckee could distract themselves with one or another bit of stimulation.

Kathleen K.

I never hurt anybody, I didn't have to sneak out the back door of a tavern because somebody walked in the front. I didn't swindle women, where ever each might be I wish her continued success, we were all in our prime and doing our own things, we had our hangups and all that, but nobody was outright out of it. One had to learn to watch her spending, little credit crises... with another, too much wine made her maudlin but she figured it out and stopped her drinking at two glasses. Was it fair we had it so easy?

Older now, each act of togetherness carries more weight, I know to savor the hugging and the rubbing and the anticipation, to be tempted by cleavage with no hope of more. Oh, how I thank the many who shared themselves with me. I also know more about other guys now and don't understand where women get the courage to hold true to themselves when men's pack mentality takes up a lot of resources admiring displays of ferocity (in war, in sport, in business). We men toss our seed here and there, we forget our duties. We endure less well, I think. Between manly-man roaring contests we're the watchful side of the race, hunters surviving by being quiet and freely-cogitating thoughts while observing the world around them. Carniverous, not seed gatherers.

↗ ⬇ ↘

Maui Wowie, that first rush of a *new* kind of kick, the top of my head lifted off and I was FREE, it was GREAT. Everything was CAPITAL. I could believe in the goodness of life and how amazing it was, REALLY, that a fern could flow. . ☐ . . . ⚡.

Don't argue nuance if you don't smoke dope, just tell me if it is commonly held that a person gets a different kind of drunk on beer or wine or hard liquor... there is a qualitative difference in the chemical reaction although all are, properly, inebriation. Just so with pot. Crops are molecularly distinct and the fact is you can have all kinds of high. Surely it is a sociable drug and a group getting high in a basement apartment has entirely different dynamics than being stoned out under the stars listening to a storm rumble in, hugging the night sky.

    Do I love it? Yes, I do. I like the parts of my personality that emerge, I like that I forget to be rigid, plodding, predictable. My associations loosen, things don't grate; nothing matches the blissful sensuality of being supremely wrecked. It is a matter of intensification through relaxation.

I have been too high.

    It is true you can smoke yourself to sleep, I'm not talking about that. I have been hurtled into weird head spaces and have trapped myself in my wonderings. There have been situations that curdled and could not be regained. Got the chemistry wrong. Thoughts are splitting, fissures in the foundation, don't like the vibe, a sour note in the smell, like bloody feet.

    More often, good times. I used to make popcorn in an old pan on the stove, melted butter and all, set up a huge tumbler of Pepsi and then I'd blow a joint while watching an old movie, enraptured by the peace I felt about my life. These midafternoon movie breaks were always done stoned, it was part of the feeling of thought travel. Some part of me is always aware that I am lucky to be alive. You too.

    I'm afraid of dying, not of being dead. I cannot imagine the force necessary to tear me from this life of mine. Ordinary life, fully my own, symbolized by a shaded parking space in the far corner of the store lot for the El Camino (Black Knight). I have the perfect spot for my vehicle, I can launch myself into the store from the same position each time. I snapped myself together during the walk across the lot, knowing the next time I went to the car I'd be driving away. The fact is, I'm half convinced I'm going to die in that car. It isn't a bad thing, it's like knowing you'll die in the house where you were born. Still, I overinsured myself just to be sure somebody else felt pain when I died— even if it was only an insurance adjuster authorizing a big check that will pass through my estate to NORML.

I don't like to drive stoned, as if my quality cannabis should be wasted to grease a weekly trip to the post office. On long road trips I'll say I've opened my eyes to the landscape's presence when I was far from populated areas. The interstate highway has some beautiful stretches of nowhere, ribbons through places nobody stops. You see a splattered creature now and then, because even birds forget to look where they're going sometimes.

LaLinda combined smoke and self-sex with me, it was apparent we were compatibly charged by marijuana and also by masturbating. In my mind, LaLinda withheld sex to teach me about desire. Nonfunctional compartments I had created in my head crashed down; I was pumping my nuts dry without a single risk, no tricks, no accidents, the unmistakable crackling energy of getting off together but still we kept deliriously apart. At first, in the dark, we didn't even see each other's outlines (that came later). Together we created a delicious ritual. We'd bake pot brownies because they gave us the longest and richest high. We'd make coffee and have ourselves a long walk while the stone "came on". We'd turn around knowing we'd be smashed before we made it back up her stairs for our dancing. Rocking together, our muscles loose from the walk, our heads light and smooth, younger and sweeter than we'll ever be again --, oh, man… we danced like lovers do. Still, when at our carnal peak, grunting and gnashing, we were blessedly free to spin, sharing the most friendly of co-orgasms. Being together enriched it, doing ourselves purified it.

↖ ⬇ ↘

I remember when it was safe(r) to talk to strangers. I used to meet new people every day. Partly this closing is symbolized by the change in drugs, the big money and artificial ego of cocaine ruined recreational drugs because people were dying (from use and from dealing). It was decreed <u>all</u> drugs are bad: it isn't true, in the sense that chugging a jug of moonshine has little to do with sampling a fine aged wine. Refining (only in the sense of reducing) the coca leaf down to rock, to crack, to instant waste… how ugly the search for sensation became. I remember the pot party era of intense mellowness turning into coke-clubs of screaming boredom. Coke-fueled alcohol seemed to be based on deception: no shots of bourbon with beer chasers, we were drinking coladas, rum & anything, and cosmic ice tea. Sweet drinks to cover the nut-numbing jolts of blow.

I backed out of that very quickly, these people wasted pot as a sedative between 'real' hits of the pow-pow-powder. Not my speed, if you'll pardon the pun. Too much money, too little high. I was going for depth and distance, not mere altitude, not the straight ups and downs of the "booster" drugs. Pot is for gliding.

LSD stayed cool for a while but it surely isn't to be mixed with an accelerant. (Which is to say no more than the amount necessary to keep you on your feet when the brain is distracted.) It wasn't hard to imagine that tripping fell out of favor with the cokers. Got harder to find because all the dough was in marching powder.

Naturally, MDA or other love drug is allied with LSD in my mind, although it is speedy as hell, because it emphasized the higher-powers of energy as might be expressed in a sensual manner. Too many experiences have convinced me that of all the drugs, I'd abuse things like MDA and LSD. I'm not a needler. Not much of a snorter. Don't believe in better living through coca-chemistry. Definite herbalist. Still loved the mindλbody benders.

⇗ ⇩ ⇘

'shrooms. /zoom\

⇗ ⇩ ⇘

If you, like me, like sex and, like me, like drugs, you may like sex on drugs, like me.
Or you might not. And that's cool too.

⇗ ⇩ ⇘

The velvet bone, the proud phallus, wee willie... *mon ami*. From my frank survey of contemporary females, I have to tell you guys that they really are NOT judging us on size alone. They can tell the difference, yes, but they usually don't accord it much value for points. (It makes sense that if something the size of a finger can stimulate a woman to orgasm then 97.634% of men have a qualified member.) Get over it, guys; relax. Be glad for what you have and use it to its best advantage because there is no reasonable way to get more. I became fond of the idea that I was more than a dick.

Being a bit of a hound, I have to take credit for many hours of peace on earth and goodwill towards men in general because of the delicate explorations I conducted with the opposing sex. I was never one to rush to judgment. You only get the first time, one time (and the second time, one time; third time, one time). There were many things I liked about women but especially I appreciated their choice in lingerie. My absolute favorite combination is a garter belt & smoky stockings with a pair of bikini briefs pulled up over them (for Stage I removal). This subdivides the thighs, rump and mound in various ways. Lord, ladies are the finest of creatures, they look like flowers but root like trees (you know what I mean, capable of cracking pavement one tendril at a time).

And that tiltable pelvis! The scooping and dipping and slamming, think of feet planted flat so the hips hop… standing then grabbing knees… one foot on the floor and one foot on a chair. Engineered by nature for maximum impact on male sensory systems.

I love the tang of women. Their products for body and face and hair and nails and skin can overwhelm— I find it murky to have sex with a woman who is clouded like that. I'm looking for a more natural sort of "aura". A trace of Ivory soap, a dot of fragrance at her pulse points, that's enough for me. Women who use heavy loads of perfume to attract men are covering the scent that would do the job for free.

The mother-load of that intimate aroma is hot wired right into the juicer. It is beyond my comprehension that each is so unique, each one unlike another, each one just right for that woman, at least for me. Why buy stuff so you smell like everybody else?

Meanwhile, down at the store, I'm thinking about the topic of work in people's lives. I hire workers who are workers. They punch in ready to go and keep going until they punch out. They are industrious and forward-thinking. They learn from experience. I don't consider somebody "hired" on their first day. I had to set up a system where the new people were able to disqualify themselves with some dignity. People say my interview technique is very direct. Why not? I may not see this person again in my life. I've got nothing to hide, the job is what it is.

Kathleen K.

I don't pay people for "being there", I pay people for "doing things." I need shelves stocked and floors mopped (never vacuumed, it's against health codes to run a traditional vacuum near food sales). The windows have to be washed, the signage changed, I need pricing and repricing. I keep the store simple so the labor savings offset the (supposed) increased sales I'd get with product-littered checkout counters and crowded-with-promotions aisleways. I run a tight warehouse so I can take advantage of bulk in nonperishables. I insist we have public lavatories— and someone has to keep those clean, after they police the employees' lounge and my conference room/office. His turn, her turn, my turn, your turn. This chore is always done at the end of your shift so you don't return to the food area afterwards. We offer a basic shower cubicle with a deep utility sink for employees' use and we're all committed to clean hands and faces. We wear store-branded ball caps which keeps us tidy and easily recognized.

I'm a believer in recognizing talent and putting it to use. Talented people are happier when they are exercising their talents. My speed demon cashiers do not enjoy culling produce, my most excellent stock guy can't bag groceries... he's a box and crate guy, he abhors bundles ("How in the hell can you pack a stack in a sack? You really need boxes with handles."). I find a person's strengths, but ask that they balance with some tasks they don't like as well.

There's lots of ways to view strangers, if you're nervous about public speaking they say to pretend your audience is in its underwear, if you are afraid of your boss imagine her as a toddler... I size up applicants by imagining them at the office window talking to strangers, how do I feel about the way they are talking to me? How do I react to this person in front of me? Are they someone I would trust? I walk them around the store, whether I think they show initial promise or not, they might need time to settle themselves in an interview situation. I keep in mind though that in retail food sales, first impressions are important. I might ask if they could suggest reasons that baked beans and refried beans are not usually shelved in the same section. If beans are together, do you include jelly beans? Coffee beans? There's no right or wrong, it addresses the way they think. I talk about schedules, short-handed is horrible in a grocery store because everything clogs at the exit which discourages people from coming in. When I take people off support duties to work the front, I'm going to have to work harder to catch up on the foregone support. I don't hire any five-day people. They get up to thirty-two hours in four days. Full benefits. This lets me sustain a larger crew (five people cover four jobs). Pick your rotation and minimize swapping. To keep quality control, all shift-trades are arranged through me in advance. If you can't give notice on missing a shift, take it off without pay and I'll give your money to one of my utility players (who cover vacations too) or from the sub sheet of people who wouldn't mind working a fifth day on short notice (costing straight-time for the store, representing extra money for them).

The secret to my success is a hand-picked, homegrown utility team. These people have worked at the store for so long they don't have to be told what to do or when to do it. They can work whenever they want to, some want a guaranteed minimum, others pick up shifts for mad money. A couple housewives, and young parents who like the obvious simplicity of the job. Punch in, work and earn, punch out. No politics, no strategy. Paid weekly.

↯ ⬇ ↘

I like to break free. That's what I appreciate about getting high. There is the distinction in state of being that washes away the straight aspects of life. The tether has been lengthened, I'm beyond my boundaries, in that rich and profuse world over the fence.

I remember explaining this to a life-long drinker who considered pot evil, yet admitted his drinking led to tunnel vision: he stared deeper and deeper into his glass, saw less and less he liked. Cannibis propelled me outward, my thoughts tilted for maximum spin, sometimes banked for long glides of knowing. I was unable to convince him to switch to my milder intoxicant. He certainly didn't sway me away from the weed.

Kathleen K.

I remember seeing stars and a harvest moon one night when I was stoned. It made me think of friendships as celestial bodies, their weight in my orbit. I thought of the passing of time as the moon striped the ocean in front of me, like it had before I arrived and would continue after my departure from these shores, from this life, this time.

Another night I was in a different country where my balcony was too high up for me to stand out on, stoned. I put a chair next to the open French doors and saw the city that way, cradled in the dense furniture on the solid floor. No stars, just a billion light bulbs, mountains bowl us in this city; out there, not far, an ocean beyond the bay. I was relaxed, out of my ordinary, in a suite with my bags unpacked. I was home away from home and I felt grand.

※ ※ ※

I met this woman, once, and only once. It was a fragrant spring evening at the Zoo where several hundred people had gathered for a fundraising walk-about when I fell into step with a small lone female. There was nothing pretentious about her, she wore tie shoes and knee socks and a denim skirt and a white cotton shirt and a suede baseball cap through which she'd pulled a short ponytail. She was older than me but, somehow, fresher.

"I say, young man, am I correct that you are alone?"

"I was up until now."

※ ※ ※

Margaret, lovely Margaret, marched me out of the Zoo after we dropped our donations into one of the dry aquariums positioned for that purpose. I took her arm feeling the first actuality of her frame. She hailed a cab to her hotel, she had explained she'd flown in from out of town for this. The Zoo, a young man… an erotic encounter without intercourse, not without satisfaction.

Margaret was not shy, she slid my hand from her knee up between soft bare thighs to her silk-covered mound. She had the cabbie take the long way and I had the joy of discovering the panties were slit for our convenience. I wasn't even kissing her, our foreheads were touching, our breath mingled, we had our eyes closed. The cabbie probably watched in the mirror but he didn't crash into anything hard enough to distract us.

She put her hand between my legs so the back of her fingers pressed against my sac, then her wrist flexed along the length of my dick. It was a perfect stop-gap action, she was acknowledging my excitement without wasting it which is how I knew there would be a rich night ahead. I reached for my wallet when the cab stopped but she shook her head and asked the doorman to have the concierge charge it with a nice tip for the cabbie and him too. We moved through the lobby unnoticed, the elevator was empty; we didn't talk because we had nothing to say to each other. Snug from the cab ride, nothing else seemed required of us. I felt her looking at me and enjoyed being admired. The body work has paid off in confidence.

The suite was large and well-appointed, I felt at ease, this was a fantasy setting and I had only to surrender. She unbuttoned her shirt while I smoked part of a joint. I gazed out the window, in no hurry, Margaret moved around, doing things that didn't relate to me. I toked along, not trying to guess where the stone was going. She took only one hit, when I was (almost) done (I always hit last and put it out properly), and that was more ceremonial than anything. Her shirt would gape open then shift shut. I saw a sheer bra and a small round belly, her hips filled the skirt and I already adored her plump thighs. To my delight, her bra had a snap front and I could loosen it without removing it, continuing to get peeks at her exciting shape. A beautiful sight, her breasts barely restrained, the bra no longer completely containing them, I saw the inside curve as her breasts rounded then peeled apart. Margaret seduced us both, conjecturing my urges.

Kathleen K.

It was getting dimmer and dimmer in the room, dusky enough to lend shape to the shadows and I granted her wish to do this in the darkening air, standing, to let our imaginations run free with just these hints. At the last moment of light she turned and flipped up her skirt, mooning me with a high proud rump that made my hands flex. I thought of thumbing those chubby cheeks apart just to hear what she'd sound like when I did. Disrobing her, I remained dressed as she had requested, loosening my pants for the same reason. We stood against each other, more and more of her flesh became available to me, and I touched and tasted it all.

Margaret was stupendous with me that night, I knew that no other man would ever have the night I had with her, she felt me all over her and I responded to that, in a way I was enthralled with the sensuality of this night, her breasts were cloud-soft and I nuzzled them with my whiskered cheek until she snatched them away from me and fondled them herself. I felt honored by her honesty, she'd pull my hands over where she wanted them, she lifted and spread to indicate her enjoyment of my sampling her, I dry humped her from behind, reaching around to joggle her dangling titties, not wanting to get in but to get near.

It was magical, I had little experience with a woman this rich, in spirit and assets, I later figured out who she was and about choked. Very blessed, properly grateful.

One night with Margaret was the sort of thing that transcends time and space, many of us hope to make these sorts of contacts in our lives. A soul from beyond our realm, not in our circle, motivated by their own expectancy. For this to happen, you must be present in the world and available to others. I would not have met Margaret in my own living room, I had to get off my ass and cross her path. I could have declined to attend the fundraiser and not been at the Zoo that night. Instead, I walked down there, and around there, just to be there. A simple agenda: drop off money:

embellished by mild exercise and sociability. That opened a link to her entirely separate from my "real" life. Or, maybe, this *was* my real life.

I love being free with a person, Margaret didn't need to know about the store or that I grew up on a farm… she knew my hands were careful with her, she knew I nipped a bit, but I had a special technique: I'd catch a bit of her flesh between my upper teeth and my tongue, so it wasn't a bite but there was pressure.

My urge for erotic adventure led me into Margaret's world and I put her to bed that night, her wildness satiated. I could see more of the real Margaret, the one who carried within her the naughty one chancing so much on the path at the Zoo, I was flattered she found me attractive. Her well-tended protoplasm was delightful, her inborn grace polished through half a century, it is my guess she would have liked the lights off no matter her age, her sensuality beckoned even in the dark.

Bad boy with good manners. Knowing my prime status: fit and free. I knew what she saw in me, educated, charitable, run-of-the-(good-)mill me. Lots of males fill the outward criteria; I gave it a conscious thought before I let this chance meeting shift to the unforgettable.

When I smoke outside, I stand still outside. Stillness feels much different than "being" outside, running errands or taking walks, because body busy-ness drowns out the world. I don't sit when I smoke. Standing still as the moon moves through pine, tip-tip-tip of rain on my hood, the rustle of a – what could it be? – a cat, a coon, a bunny-bear! – in the overgrowth. I am less intrusive to the environment, I slip into shadow and am embraced like a temporary tree, rooted for the moment, life moving around it and within it but it is not moving.

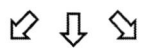

Kathleen K.

I'm buying my pot from a pro, there is an underground and I'm sticking to the tidy part of it. I'm not driving a 4x4 out to an island with $13,000 in cash… somebody my guy knows knows somebody who does that part. I get mine in slim rolls, baggied. No short counts from either of us. I bring the cash and get the stash.

Time was, we'd practically be shoveling the stuff, it was abundant, voluminous, not the tight buds of today. We were not surprised the government tried to suppress it but ganga was closer to cognac on the intoxication continuum. It was inherently liberating from the very realities The Man promoted: straight jobs and paying taxes and caring about sewer referendums. No time for dancing in the mist, no, no, no, you freaking freaks— do something useful.

Ridicule of and indifference to "the important things"— that behavior can't be allowed by people who think their way of life is *important*. Pot got linked to hippies which meant college kids which meant the squandering of the ruling class's investment in propagating their own faith to another generation. Enforce the ban! Declare war on drugs! Punish the children for not being what we expected them to be. We've given them everything we wanted to give them. Can't they appreciate that? Bust those thankless little shits.

↗ ⬇ ↘

We'd do our pot deals in mall parking lots, I'd hop into my buddy's car where the package awaited in a shopping bag. I left the money on the seat when I got out on the other side of the lot. Zip. Quick. Nothing fancy. Commerce.

Dry spells are rare because I've learned to avoid them. I can keep to the essence of being stoned and not indulge so much in lean times. I husband my stock, buying ahead when the grass is available, hiding a bit here in my hollowed-out copy of <u>Crime and Punishment</u>, the polar packs in the freezer (guaranteed dry inside for 180 days). I keep a roach pot and dip into it for potent, resin-laced combinations with weak pot I'm stringing along.

It's like mixing drinks, concocting sensuous food. You realize that this stuff is grown on patches of earth under the sun (or a lab-like simulation of that patch)— every crop seeding its own peculiar photocellular concoction.

I'm hoping that the study of bioscience will continue to lead the way to understanding the chemical actions of a life. Insulin is an example, people DIED because they couldn't figure out sugar caused a reaction in the pancreatic system. Figuring out dirty hands were bad for wound care: big lesson. I'm hoping various research projects will explain *how* pot does what it does.

THC is dangerous to play with (so is surfboarding, skiing, parachuting, jaywalking, etc.). You make decisions in life, you'll skip that dental exam, blow off the insurance agent… inhale some smoke. I'd like better information on the subject to circulate, information we stoners deserve to have. Some things are true about pot intoxication: not good to drive on, do not pretend you're working when high. The good thing about it being illegal: you have to respect it. You might get casual about cracking a beer at lunch once in a while but keep the herb for when you want to get gone.

Weed works well with my personality, I'm not given to fits of temperament and have no seething secret hatred of humanity to unleash. I would take a joint out to the beach on a rainy afternoon when the straights were inside keeping dry. It's a challenge to keep the doobie going in the wind but it's worth the effort. The water, the sky, the cackle between them. I'm so far gone from my world that I'm out of time yet firmly traversing place. My heels leave marks in the sand, I dig deeper and deeper, considering unnamable things, letting the world spin beneath my boots, my current self the center of all space as far as I can ever know.

I remember one night, long long ago, LaLinda and I were pursuing relationships with others, and it hurt me to be happy around her. I got the impression things might not be going as well for her as they were for me.

She asked me to take a walk with her and I dreaded having to reject whatever idea she had to get us back together. Instead, she talked to me about sex with men. She wanted me to explain to her how it worked from the "other" side, was it really so much the *act* and not the purpose. For me, the *act* is in and of itself stupendous. Yes, aside from its many purposes, the *act* mattered.

Shining our flashlights ahead on the path, I asked her a few questions of my own. Why did women not believe the evidence that men needed women and wanted them? We seemed sincerely drawn to them. Accept it for the cosmic mystery it is and enjoy it. There are lots of guys and not all of them carry tape measures in their heads. Some like the sound of a throaty laugh in their ear and the gossamer of girl where others see the social shield. We like it when we get basic and FEEL. Translating FEELINGS into language may not be our post-coital forte but, coitally, we're rendering. Cut back on the talk-talking, too, it's simply too much information for guys to process. Let us look at you, we find that pleasant.

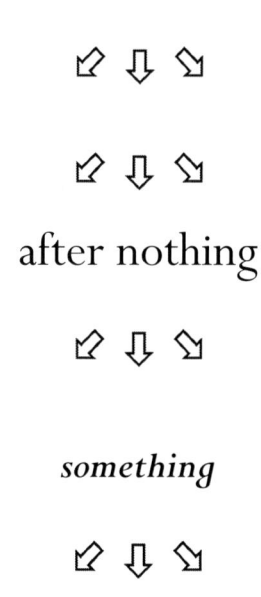

after nothing

something

Here's a stoner thing. I used a sturdy shoe box for my paraphernalia but the most convenient drawer to keep the box handy was just barely deep enough for it. I'd have to pull the drawer out almost all the way to pop the top on the box, I did that for months, every trip to the box irked me. Then I realized the drawer was <u>wide</u> enough to accommodate the box sideways. I could slide the drawer open less than half-way and flip the top off into the waiting space between the box and the desk. A system was born!

I've suffered spills (pot spills). Worse when you're straight, of course, because it is all so clear when it happens. One minute, you've got your stuff, and the next minute it is dematerializing into the carpet and between floorboards and through the upholstery.

There's a fine line between salvage and lint. There is the financial side, the stuff costs money so you don't like to toss it away. There's the unborn dreams, unthought ideas… never-had laughs.

For a long time, LaLinda was my feminine ideal precisely because I did not know her as well as I thought. Her body was all the counterpoise I'd ever needed for my masculinity. Her legs were well-formed and shapely, from ankle to hip. She had flanks, if you know what I mean, a long sweep of flesh into the rise of her bottom. I considered hers the first truly heart-shaped ass I'd gotten my hands onto. Her small waist seemed the essence of femininity, I didn't leech her sensuality, it went way beyond that. I condemned many other women to stand up to my projections about LaLinda before I learned the truth. The fact is there are great bodies and LaLinda got one but most of the rest of us are ordinary. It's why some of us model skimpy bathing suits and most don't. I never got over marveling at her but, then again, I wasn't supposed to. I was encoded with the gene that said, 'give yourself to the best'.

Then you gotta talk about Bonnie. Bonnie was a drinker. I learned how different that was, over time, we were inebriated in separate ways. I'd turn on some music, hit the bong then crawl all over Bonnie. She'd numb herself out and let me do whatever I wanted. It was like being in a playground for me. Women rarely lend themselves to that one-sided of a sex relationship and I found myself learning the secrets of the clitoral orgasm.

Oblique.

Bonnie was thin, she ran four miles during the day as atonement for drinking the night before. I once suggested she run at night instead of drinking and she thought I was being droll. In my appreciation for the great latitude granted me sexually, I didn't pick up on the fact she didn't do much for me. A little head, balling dog style. She spread, she'd cross closed over my hand, no end of the positions she'd assume so I could get at her. She'd rock her hips when I fingered her, reach back and spread herself so I could twist my way deeper inside. She wasn't the cuddly type but she was responsive. By accident I learned to rub her pussy lips together around her clit and a magician was born. I have not met one single female who didn't melt with that technique. It's not really a trick, it is a knowing.

Bonnie had also introduced me to the concept of needing a brain in a woman. We didn't talk much once we got loaded. The result was primarily sexual and I surprised myself by thinking, after a good long while, that (maybe) unlimited sex wasn't enough.

Bonnie didn't argue at my going, there'd be another guy. She did think I had done an especially good job and promised to think about me while the next guy bunged her.

My secret vice is pain pills, I love the stuff doctors give if you tell them codeine kills your stomach. I hoard the extras from any legitimate script (asking for more but in truth needing less than average). I swallow one of those goodies every now and then. Sleepy, floating, disengaged -- loosed. I especially like them about an hour before bed, so I can feel the world slip away, and I approach my clean sheets numbed and blunted. I bat my cock around, not intending anything to happen, lacking the "burn" to do it, recollecting incidents as my dick gets thick, hazy on the details, congested. There is no clear division between being awake and being asleep. I pool quietly, cock in hand, dense.

I would take the heavy strands of long hair from the crown of her head and start a braid, I plaited it to her skull by taking another section from side to side, until her luxurious hair ran like a ribbon down the back of her head, along her nape. Her face was revealed, her high forehead, her wide eyes, her savory lips. I would watch her kissing and licking my crotch, not just the rod but the groin, the base, the root. She seemed so purely feminine, ministering to me, hunched over her own sex, but her scent was in the air; I could feel her gathering mass.

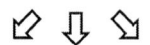

Kathleen K.

I used to hate those cash registers that figured out the change because it seemed insulting to the checker but now I'd rather machines passed out the cash because people simply cannot handle money. It amazes me that a simple exchange of paper (dollars for receipt) causes such confusion. People lose the ability to count to ten or multiply to a hundred. They can't hold a stack of bills and find a place for three coins. I reward the workers who realize there is a technique for handling money. Routine. Habit. Drill. Focus. Every transaction is simple, there is at some point a total of money exchanged, that is a finite fixed fact around which the rest should be built. Pay attention to the money. It's the fairest thing you can do for the customer.

I take accuracy over personality at the register because I put the personality on bag service. [It also diverts the customer from distracting the checker which increases accuracy.] We bag right. We use bag science. We know our bags and how to achieve a carry-able parcel. Packers are puzzle-fiends. They will understand how to get a head of damp lettuce, a loaf of bread in a waxed paper sack, a can of air freshener and six candles into your hands safely, and that package will last until you get home.

When duty calls, every employee bags but the best make it a pleasure to deliver all the buyer's new stuff in transportable form.

I like the grade school kids who come to the store; some of them are discerning judges of product and converse with me regarding supply and demand. One suggested I raise part of the candle bin so the grown-ups could smell them too. She was right. I've lowered some of the scales in produce and fruits for young and old alike, got a few more small gardening tools because they're a kid favorite. I'm rarely wistful about not being a father, I don't "feel" it in me, I'm not against it in theory but in practice I'm careful to avoid it.

Kids are a sub-species of the humanoic cluster we call "man", they impress me most of all with their clarity of thought. You might not, at first, see the connections; kids are following their ideas as they take shape, they haven't taught themselves to not take notice of the obvious.

My marketing experts didn't think to put "baby wipes" in the adult toiletries but moist towelettes move quickly there. Those things are handy in the car, in the bedroom, in the lounge… We combine a family of food products so you can get corn chips, salsa, beans, rice and tortillas in one place. These cap the islands at the back, we know they're popular because they have to be restocked frequently. Then, for traditionalists, we've got all the chips in one location, all the legumes in others. It isn't that much harder to stock for the customers' convenience. I paid a college student to draw a master plan of empty shelving as it sits in the store (each aisle has six sections), we keep magnified copies listing all the current content categories displayed on the four walls of the store for staff and customers.

You can divide people into list shoppers and free shoppers. The list people most likely know the store and have their targets arranged accordingly, grouping items for logical access. Free shoppers wander here and there, they require more assistance, they miss some of the bargains. You get to know your hybrids too, the organized mom with a cartful of her weekly rations might be seen occasionally raiding the pizza and ice cream freezers for a quick meal, grabbing a pair of panty hose and a jar of pickles on her way out. I try to anticipate the market trends but am best served by keeping my eye on the simple details. Keep the shelves stocked, the prices prominent, and move people through checkout.

We don't sell tobacco or liquor to minors, we closely inspected all ID. We earned our reputation at the local high schools as a place not to go for beer and wine, cigarettes (suspicious amounts of toilet paper or eggs) which is exactly correct.

↗ ⇩ ↖

Hypocrite? I don't think so. What is hard to describe to the people who hate drugs is that pot is distinct, in the same way 3.2 beer is unlike "real" alcohol let alone fortified wine. Marijuana never should have been tarnished with the bad-drugs reputation; this mistake makes it too easy for kids to dismiss the necessary warnings about cocaine and speed, and glue-sniffing for that matter. Don't get me started on prescription drugs. Alcohol is a problem because it's portrayed as a social lubricant, pot is a problem because it is wrongly portrayed as *bad* when mostly it is *naughty*. It's best reserved for the mature, as are all indulgences. It is a matter of choice, it is a matter of philosophy and intent, it is pipe-grade tobacco with a sustaining wave. I have decided it is a private thing, like lovemaking, and should be considered under the "consenting adults/closed doors" clause. Not for freeway use, not at the city park— confined to private gatherings on personal property.

↗ ⇩ ↘

There have been times when the sex is good, even great, but still there is no growth or hope of growth. It is an odd thing to find yourselves having intensely resplendent emotions and then moving on, amiable and grateful and not at all in love. There is a post-60's free love explanation yet the problem is ages old, because coupling calls out all elements of the self including the jovial sexkateer.

The surrender of physical separateness! Scientists have measured "personal space" and know there are biochemical reactions in its breach. Poets and painters portray it. To stand close, to brush against, to touch, to feel as you are felt... intensified as it becomes full body contact, reverberating with intromission. We are, foremost, thinkers, but our foundations are solidly of the flesh. We get information from an arched brow, a tilted head, licked lips. Amusement is peculiar to humans, some higher animals can express a preference and appreciate a surprise but (to our current knowledge) they do not sit back and chuckle over some previous scenario let alone write a screenplay about it. Laughter has evolved from the same urge to show teeth for defense purposes: it is an acknowledgement, touché. We can make wry comments about casual intercourse but there remains the fact that to have good, let alone great, sex you must have a regard for yourself and for the other.

⬈ ⬇ ⬊

 Fucking is over-rated... it isn't *everything* although it is <u>something</u>. Balling, rutting, getting the go: whatever you call it. It is a part of sex. I'd need to invent an orgasmometer to prove my belief that women's pleasure is stupendously more complex than the men's (which may be why men believe we need it more often than women). I'm not going to bother hoping the world is ready to admit the basic backwardness of sexual theory in general. Men may hunt for mates but they are fooling themselves if they think they pick their own targets. Some of the culling is done early, you don't even realize it. From the minute one sperm achieves the egg, you've got the DNA equivalent of a score card. From the astrological facts at birth you've got cultural significance (date, time, latitude and longitude combine to a specific stroke of time at a specific spot on earth) [would it be more interesting if you could base personal astrology on the true moment of conception?]. How much does your family, neighborhood, culture influence? It determines the available gene pool.

 I love screwing, banging, riding the tide, hopping the bunny, undulating in unison. Silken soft sensuous sweet, imperious. The intimacy is based, in part, on revealed appetite— I <u>do</u> want to do you, I <u>do</u> want to do that, I <u>do</u>, I do, *I* **am**.

 Do me. Please. Do to me. Give me. Grant me. Have me. Please, me.

⬈ ⬇ ⬊

 When you want what is offered, you have terrific energy being exchanged, and energy is expressed as heat. The sheen of desire. I remember this when I masturbate, which is dry-ice sex. I like the sharp and almost acrid sense of male sex, it harmonizes with the richer, fertile smell of a hot female and is harder to track during intergenderation. Alone, even when invoking the most significant of man-woman union, there remains the solo sense of re-creation. The surge of male ego makes my bones sweat sex.

Sometimes I remember a certain twitch of the lip because it was involuntary, it was pure reaction, it spoke of the unconscious and the subconscious. I know there is subterfuge between lovers, there are secret thoughts and unspoken triggers. She doesn't have to be faking it to decide to trill a little; sometimes the grunts and groans are for your own benefit. Even erections and moist vaginas don't mean true love, these are physiological and psychological indicators. It is the essence of mutual lust to provoke hotter responses, the hunger is hormonal, pheromonal, you are affected beyond reason, you become impassioned, the room spins, the moments are distorted because the feelings don't process in real time. There are twinklings of naked souls, ageless.

Who makes me think this way? Judith.

The calmest years were with Judith; she never loved me. Judith felt sex was a natural function that had to be performed routinely, Wednesdays were good for her, so she engaged in a thorough sex workout with me once a week. I remember I was just getting the store going the way I wanted it. I didn't have a big enough team to pull it off, I had to make up a lot of the slack myself, but my ideas were right and they showed promise. I saw Judith on Wednesdays. It meant I didn't have to freak about being the single usher at my friends' weddings, the odd chair at dinner. (I have a secret lover.) The bit of a "crowd" I had once enjoyed was peeled apart as houses were built and families were started. I didn't want that right now; I wondered if I ever would. Judith made me understand that I could be connected without the conventional burdens. For reasons left undetailed here, her emotional needs were stretched in another direction (filial duty) and she could make room for only one liaison in her life at this point. It would be cruel to dangle a future when all she had was the conviction that her Wednesday evenings away from home were necessary. She had no time for movies or dinners out, she cabbed to a nearby park and we took a little walk to provide a transition into our togetherness. By the time we got to my place we were loose, relaxed, at ease. It wasn't so much that we didn't have a future, we had to sink into our private emotions to do what we did. There was no room for social concerns, we were carefree in our expressiveness. Promise existed between us, we got to experience the clear sense of equals, nothing stopped our powerful sexuality from twining and climbing.

Judith was medium sized, with an angular face softened by naturally curly hair. I think of her with her eyes closed, mouth open slightly. She liked to lay back with her arms above her head, if she was on top she leaned far forward. She felt completely open to me in that position, her heart exposed. I'd shove her breasts together and lick their tips while she ground her crotch against my thigh, using her powerful ass to shift her cunt forward and back. In all my life, Judith alone made me berserk for sex. I'd be panting, begging, and still she would hold herself away from me, I'd demand that she stop tormenting me. Even dogstyle, I couldn't get into Judith until she made it so. Holy fucking Lord. Getting into that woman was a spinal tap, I collapsed into a tubular projection and shoved my whole self into her. Meta-physical! She had a muscular vagina, it was a wonder. Her sexiness was partly due to her serious nature, she sensibly used every body part to its purpose. This prolonged my pleasure immensely because she changed into so many states while I kept stiff and hard. She had a pronounced vestibule, you could slip your cock between her legs and snuggle into a damp grotto, superbly fashioned from her deep pelvis. She would flex her thighs and clench her butt and you felt like you were *almost* inside her – so close. You'd pop the head in easy enough but then there was the dense sense of woman and my cock would halt. She had to let me in, do that thing that opens her up to me.

Judith was astounding in bed, I didn't want to lose her trust, and somewhere deep inside herself she held me at bay. She couldn't have been so free with me if I had pushed myself forward. I was able to admire her without defining her. I used my dripping cock to write it on her (symbolically)… "Nothing matters but this between us."

Sometimes we were taking turns, not really saying so, but she'd lick my dick so I'd suck her pussy, if she presented herself for rear entry I was to take her in my lap next time. You work these things out over time and it helps establish balance.

I was three inches taller and forty pounds heavier, her proportionately long legs and short torso caused me to hunch when I got on top of her, she was the sort of partner you wanted to cover with your body, to make the most contact. I'd lay her on top of me just to feel the distinctive body alignment, amazed at how close she could feel.

She liked to spoon, my cock pressed to her backside, my right arm over her ribs so I could fondle her front. She said nobody had ever handled her breasts like I did. I'd stretch out the nipples between my knuckles (it makes for a much softer grip than the fingertips), I would thumb her nipples inward which she found immensely erotic. I took my time hefting her hardening tits, they seemed to tighten for the sole purpose of displaying her nips.

When erect, the crowns flushed a shade or two darker and the centers firmed. I'd sense the transformation, I'd feel it between my lips. She would watch me suckling, bemused and aroused by my avid hunger for her. It might seem I was totally intent on her teat but in fact I sensed the parting of her legs, the planting of her feet, her every movement was known to me. Still, I confess I am a suckaholic and would nurse at the tit for a long period of time.

Judith liked to get stoned with me although she swore it had never done much for her in the past. I didn't dispute her because she was right, some people don't get off easy. For her, trust was necessary. A raucous party with strangers wasn't going to put her at ease. She wouldn't join my high until we'd had our first sex of the evening, I guess she didn't want to risk the essential purpose which, once achieved, left us open to each other. More importantly, after sex, she felt strong within herself. Pot actually did have a very potent effect on her and she sensibly mistrusted that. It was fun to fill a small pipe for her and watch just a few wisps of smoke curl in her head, she was charmingly vague after she got off, tilting her head a bit. Her eyes narrowed but she didn't squint.

I bought her a short nightgown on an impulse since we normally didn't do gifts. The fabric was dark red with thin black shoulder straps. It clung at the chest and encased her torso then flared slightly over the hips so it would swirl around her thighs when she moved. It was very flattering to her body type and I could tell she felt good in it. I couldn't have put it into words but she exhibited it to me one night, rising to her feet to demonstrate its styling. A satisfied feeling filled my heart, she was truly happy at that moment. She said I made her feel noticed.

I wanted her, yes. I wanted her in my arms, on my sheets, within my heart. I felt a big love for her, the kind that doesn't involve a mortgage. I loved that such a pretty woman would be flattered by my attentions, I loved that such a smart woman would argue with me like she did— naked. Her physical features pleased me, her soul was clear, I could see her glory. I felt she treated me like a man, she was playful without being a tease.

I swear that we'd all be better off if we each had a steady supply of affirmation such as I shared with Judith. Maybe she and I had created an island of unreality, when our commitments were set aside and we digressed into a pocket of self-hood not usually given enough attention. Maybe it was redemptive. How truly I admired Judith, how carefully I tended our relations. I remember mockingly intoning, "I am not worthy," and her seriously agreeing. "No one really <u>deserved</u> the love of another, we were lucky to have connected." Perhaps she was right, who could say it was fair that I ended up with the most luscious females, one after another it seemed. I was an average guy lucking into great women. (It probably helped that I wasn't living family style or in love with my car or otherwise distracted.)

Judith taught me about paying attention. I started to buy her panties, knowing she preferred a full backside although she didn't mind the tiniest triangle in front, many featured slits in the crotch. She had the mistaken belief I'd be less excited by her butt if it the skin wasn't showing. My enjoyment of her bottom made her nervous, even though I had reassured her I only wanted the cheeks; I knew she'd never surrender to sodomy so why spook her by asking? My hands cupped and jiggled her buns, using all my self control to steer clear of her Do Not Disturb zone. We both pretended she didn't grind against my palms when we were doing it the regular way, nothing was said of her settling her buttocks into my flexing hands as I guided myself into her vagina.

Yes, a thong would have flattered her but the eroto-psychic price was too high, making her self-conscious didn't serve either of us. The indulgence of dressing her up was something that gave us structure. We kept a small trunk with her treasures in it, I'd put new things on top of it when she came to visit. These weren't expensive items yet they established the courting gestures, we shared a sense of anticipation.

For me, she indulged in my preference for "scenarios." I'd ask to be allowed to discover her bathing in my tub, could she be on the floor in front of the television watching a wretchedly romantic old movie while I rubbed her back? We'd play strip scrabble. Silly, stoned friends making love. My fantasies were acted out, she found it fascinating that such things mattered to me. No matter how it started, she wanted to be held tight and taken deeply. Sexy Judith, held fast by one devotion, still able to spill the very essence of her sex into my waiting hands. I never felt so at peace with any other person. There was nothing between us but mutual admiration and gratitude to the Unseen Powers that it was possible to make this sort of liaison mean something.

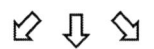

Must not fail to mention the Club Years. Like many red-blooded American guys, I spent a cycle of my life going to taverns and dance places, tangled in drugs and booze, getting it on with strangers I'd never see again, plus my regulars, girls I'd run into once in a while and we'd do it because the last time was fun so why not? Much of the detail is lost because I was addled at the time but I prefer to remember the resilient youthfulness of it. We were fresh. Much to my surprise, I never got used to being naked with a female. It excites me every time. Drunk, stoned, blasted— naked still tingled.

Not all of the sex was terrific. Sometimes I would forget what I was doing, not sure if I was starting or finished. Of course, at that age the loop ran much faster. I'd do it in the car, at a beach, in a garage; I'd drop to my knees and nuzzle a crotch in the parking lot behind a bar. Hey, people, getting turned on was a natural force and I decided I was powerless to deny my manly sexuality. It insisted on rearing its ugly head.

One older woman slipped $100 into my jacket pocket, and I thought I could do it but Johnny was not on the spot. This turned out to our advantage because she actually just wanted to hold a young man to her shoulder and hum to herself. I passed out and she cradled me for an hour. She shooed me out the door, relaxed and grateful. I understood the money was incidental and that I'd been valued for my size and shape, for the disarmament of my sex, rewarded because I was a few evolutionary steps above hugging a pillow yet man enough not to say so outloud.

Kathleen K.

"We're balls of energy, like sparks rising up out of a bonfire, we're alive while we're burning, arcing out at birth then falling, falling back to the fire."

"A pool of energy… we're droplets thrown off a cresting wave, warmed in the sun then dropping back through the surface to the churning below."

"Exactly."

It was no exaggeration that I was a stoner with a boner, I was ready to party with the people. I couldn't see any reason to be worried about growing up. That happened to other people, people who forgot what it felt like to up-end a beer outside an old barn on an autumn night, facing various strangers. Nothing fazed/phased me. If two sisters wanted to share me, that was OK. In that particular situation, I felt a little left out at times, they had some fun with me but their focus was all in the family. It has remained a powerful memory even though, at the time, I was irked that they spent so much time on each other. Now I remember how one suckled on the other; I see them, thighs parted, fingers fucking the other. They had been right all along, they didn't need me at that point. They ignored my petty jealousy and gave me a once in a lifetime opportunity that has grown in value over the years. (In this sense, they were smart to pick me because I remain reverent.)

There is fluidity between women. Even porn seems softer when the females are working each other. Buck, ram… male. Intercourse involves a prong of some sort, an intrusive, invasive weapon of conquest. It has to be buried in something to work, it needs a target to complete its function. Women open themselves (and each other, I know now). There can be as much strength, as much power, as much assertion, but in the end it is the curves and softnesses that make each woman memorable. They coax forth the sounds of life, moans and growls and a gasping laugh you only hear at the height of sensual culmination.

That's the stoner part talking... the ability to step back and experience all the senses not just the prick-ly one. When I'm running on pure male hormones, I am the prong! I don't have eyes for detail, I don't taste the waiting. Especially with pot, I'm able to dissociate from the conquest impulses. I'm the first to admit that sex is more powerful than I can handle. There have been times I can't even remember what we were doing when we did it once it was done. I feel the slide of my cock, I hear distant shouting (hers? mine?) and my body twists to gain the maximum sensation, who can believe the variations on the old in-out? Pot is a filter, allowing me to accumulate energies that would simply shoot out and be gone if I didn't cloud my event horizon. It is very easy to become fixated on the simple goal of getting in then getting off then getting away. Marijuana leads to lingering. The herb makes nipples delicious. Nothing like being naked and doing a doobie. Bong. Bong. Bong.

I keep thinking about those sisters. I can't prove they were sisters, because I didn't actually know them, and they didn't look like sisters, but we all know that can happen in families. They were partying in a bar, playing pool and flirting. I was what they were looking for, I felt them pick me out when I came in the back door. I was lonesome and looking for company and spent a while wondering which one might actually want me until I picked up the share-and-share-alike plan. They didn't want anybody too drunk, that's why they intercepted me at the door (they said). I got up to go outside for a little buzz, although neither cared to join me smoking. It gave me something to do while I figured out how to get started with two girls. You open your arms as wide as you can and say, "Come on over here, lovelies." One, two, three— you're connected.

It was almost too much for me, my eyes wanted to go in different directions, my hands weren't enough to hold them. I had to shut down, turn off my interpretive mind, collect information and savor the sensations. The small brunette had pointy tits, I remember them against my back while she slipped her hand up along my cock and stroked her sister's face as that one ate me. It was the only time I was at the center (in the middle) and after that I got one then the other girl as she did what she pleased to her inverted partner. The blond was hugely sexual, I would have gone for her first, she had deep cleavage and a high round rear, I liked her roughness. She pushed her dark haired sister open and grabbed at her thighs, leaving finger mark like the echo of a shout, insisting the sister liked it that way even as that sister breathed, "no, please, no" then gushed.

She may have protested but she certainly responded to rough stimulation, she was wet and juicy and ready to go, I had two fingers deep inside her while she jacked off on my hand, her breasts being pinched and jiggled by her sister; I didn't want to interfere, I had all I could handle feeling her pussy clamp down on my fingers, she was sucking my hand deeper into her. I relished her.

Due to my position, I couldn't really <u>see</u> how the blond ate the other but I did notice she moved her head more than I moved mine and I realized I had a bit more to learn. It also dawned on me that she didn't accelerate to match her partner's excitation. She kept steady on, steady on, while climaxes came and went, yet the underlying foundational basis of their connection grew hotter and hotter. They both screamed out, sharply, and I felt a flush of sex. One gigantic stereo-rotic head fuck.

↗ ⇩ ↘

It all comes together for me. I see people on TV being miserable and I wonder, how do you do that to yourself? How do you fail to realize you have one life to live? Get off your butt and do what you want to do, what you have decided you need to do. Motivational seminars are necessary because people have forgotten you are <u>supposed</u> to be productive, you are charged as a sentient being with contributing to our environment (or, at least, at first, to do no harm). Arrange your day how ever you like but, once arranged, get on with it.

The store is so real, there's no better place for me to be during my work day. I don't have to wonder if I'm doing my job because it shows. It redeems the hedonist side of me that wants to party. It balances and that is good. I want to go on the record as a libertarian in that regard, do your duty then you are free. Contribute to the common good and then pursue personal happiness and liberty. Hold true and steady when you're on the job then relax and give over to your own time, your private time, the time that, finally, is your life. I am not being facetious here. Are you straight with yourself and your goals? If you want a family are you putting in the time to make it successful? If you want to fly are you signed up for flight school? I don't think you should waste your time regretting the undone. Spend your time doing things.

Get in some habits. I walk forty-five minutes every other day. Rain, shine, snow. I don't even wonder why I do it any more. It is just something that I do. I don't do it for fitness, contemplation, or other describable motive. I do it because I've done it for so long that I am uneasy if I don't do it.

Another thing about those sisters. I knew I was being stupid even as I resented them not doing enough things to me. In all my fantasies of a three-way, I'd been at the center, the young god to two adoring angels, the hung stud to a pair of mares, not even considering the motivation of the women in my fantasies. My eyes were peeled open and pinned back. I was forced to see how one-sided I'd been. I spot this trait in lots of guys, they're convinced the women are satisfied by mere proximity to the male. She is believed to be honored and fulfilled by his pleasure. No. It seems they have a few demands of their own.

I was never as rough as these two girls were with each other, but I knew I could be more emphatic than I had been. I loved seeing them devour each other's boobs, sucking noisily, twisting and pinching. They vocalized, sounds with few words, short words: yes, yes, oh, yes, oh, no, nO, NO… NO, No, no, noooo… oh.

Then there is the matter of their backsides. They didn't play with each other's, which surprised me at first, until I figured out the simple fact they were anal takers, not givers, and I found my niche(s), as it were.

I had the women face each other and embrace, then I straddled their knees so I could reach a bum on each side. It was an awkward angle but I took my time, letting them have the comfort of the familiar fronts while I began my grooming of their tails.

I had them belly to belly, as I lubricated them, violating their privacy. They had become separate beings again, the dual-anal stimulation powerful (because rare) worked with each individual— and must have resonated as each accompanied the other in frottage. In truth, I kept adding lubricant to my fingers even after the sisters were relaxed. I gasped at the surge of machismo when I felt these women rear up against my hands, offer more of their secrets to me. I was going to do one, or both, anally. One was, or both were, going to let me.

The blond invited me to nudge her, just that, but nudge with the soft fat head of my real live cock, let her feel the knock at her back door, slip in the head and let her pucker tight under the rim while I count to thirty, that's all I do, I don't move and I count to thirty, slowly. I let her feel the outrage, the excited realization that I'm in her bung. I'm in her. I give her a deep application of lubrication then I nudge a little deeper and count a little slower. I get buried and hold it. She's gripping the hand of her sister, and I feel her relax, there is a lessening of tension and I'm welcome, I'm accepted, she has taken me and with care I am fully inside her, I have sodomized us all. I didn't do the other one, I couldn't, I was caved in. It was a rare enough treat on its own, but to be done with a witness opened another dimension.

I loved being watched, I loved watching. I hadn't understood how very much I observed the human condition and was drawn to the acting out of emotions. If I noticed a couple arguing on the street, I didn't turn away. I watched, and saw myself in one or both of them. You don't need a sound track for a good argument, especially if the people are standing so you get full-scale body language. It's raw emotion crackling between two electri-bio forms.

I had to leave the sisters, entangled in each other's arms, almost asleep, grateful to me for enacting one scene in their lifelong play, me post-orgasmic, at one with the world, not looking for trouble.

I ceremonially emptied my roach pot from time to time, handling the marijuana butts collected from a variety of weeds, some so short they were not worth unrolling but would be, instead, scissored resinous paper and all. The big ones I snip in half length-wise then empty of the thickened weed, noticing different generations of my pot: the leafy green with the mild high, the darkly rich sticky ends of mind-blowing jade-green exotic. Some red thread.

I returned at least a third of them to the kitty, it is wise to hold back a portion even when you don't see the need because the need <u>will</u> arise. Then you mix in an equal measure of some old-faithful so it would smoke smooth.

I'd been getting the same kind of pot for months, it was reliable and I wouldn't complain, but I was in the mood for some different stones and mixing it with roaches would do the trick. My head wanted to travel new roads.

I got out some old pictures, that was deliberate on my part. I want some portion of me to stay in tune with the past so I set aside an evening once in a long while to look at my history, remember the people who have been so important to me, and I always end up thanking them I've gotten this far.

Windstorm, uprooted tree kills car driver. Bridge malfunction, woman dies. Peanuts in neighbor's cookies kill a visitor. None of these people woke up that day expecting to meet death, they were having their ordinary lives, they weren't being treated for illness or undertaking dangerous missions. Going to work, coming home, visiting next door... and I didn't want to forget that.

⇗ ⇩ ⇘

A friend of mine was raped and murdered. She hitchhiked to her death, the random mischance of saying yes to a killer's ride. I can't stand to FEEL the full weight of the horror of that. My friend was punched, kicked, whipped, raped, stomped, peed on, throttled, revived, raped, strangled, defiled. I have read all the books about her killer and not one justified the horror, this opportunistic destroyer of life may have been twisted by his childhood but as a man he pitted his brooding 218 pounds against the smallest of adversaries. I wish these guys would go after the "male model abuser" so often at the root of these stories. If you can't keep from killing to the detriment of society at least stalk your fellow wife beaters and child molesters to society's betterment, twisted ego to twisted ego— up the ante then go ahead and play to win. Tackle a "real" (man) target if you dare to claim that's the proof of your he-man power.

I learned about women's fear of men and still struggle to understand how it happens this way. Women have tangible obstacles to living in peace; this isn't feminist rhetoric, it is statistical and cross-cultural. We're raised to think certain things, overtly by our parents and teachers, haphazardly by our experiences in life. Size and nature play a role in dominance but the male's dogged need to be king of the pile is hollow when it comes at the price of women and children – who exactly do we think we are we saving the world *for*?

⇗ ⇩ ⇘

Still, I'm not a peace-nik, hippy dippy. The facts of my life make it easy for me to survive and even succeed. Inside me, though, there is a fighter, and I know I'd be capable of standing forward if duty called. I learned this in the parking lot of an Albertson's grocery. I saw a situation that nobody else seemed to notice, a short bored toddler widening the distance between herself and her distracted mother who was gathering up the scattered contents of a broken grocery bag, a teenage driver intent on a parking space that had just opened up nearby. Time slowed as I swooped forward and snatched the little girl in one hand and lifted her above my shoulder. Her mother screamed at me, terrified I was grabbing her child, as the car shuddered to a stop near my left hip. I had *zoomed* to reach that kid. In later years, I would read about this super-strength phenomenon: it most often occurs for altruistic reasons (to save a man pinned beneath a fallen tree, to free a trapped woman in a sinking car…), bursts of energy that would burn us up if sustained, but delivered like a jolt to let us reach through time, as it is measured by humans, and do in seconds what hours couldn't force. You cannot summon it to open a vault for money, it makes you jump in an icy river to save a plane crash victim, it makes you act beyond your conscious desire.

I was reassured of my humanity. I hadn't even stopped to think I might be hurt, I simply could <u>not</u> allow that car to touch that child without going through me first. I wanted the kid to live, I wanted the young driver to have a future, I wanted that mother to forgive herself for chasing a $2 can of beans at the risk of her priceless child. I didn't have to wonder what I was doing. It was the right thing to do. I did it instinctively. I was given a gift that day, too. I knew myself.

↗ ⬇ ↘

That's how I got started in the grocery business, by the way. The owner of the store gave me a gift certificate that I traded in for a job bagging groceries until promoted to supervising the load porch. Shoppers could take a tag number from the cart(s) containing their purchases. They could go to their cars and drive around to the covered porch to have the bags loaded into the car. The loading clerk matched the cart tags, the cool dry bags were as carefully loaded as they had been packed. Maybe the customer had a few quick errands to be done before the bags were picked up. That was part of the service. Food valets.

                                                ↗ ⬇ ↘

   How about this one? I had a girlfriend who liked to fall asleep while we had sex. It wasn't that she was bored, she finally convinced me, but she felt a rush of trust as her mind spun down. I sucked little hickeys on the underside of her breasts, we agreed I could finger her but not use a toy, I could mount and penetrate her but not climax inside, I could come next to her but not upon her. We only did this sometimes, maybe once every five sex episodes.

   It was an adventure because she truly was asleep, lightly drifting while I stroked her cinnamon skin. She had a little pot belly that made her seem innocent, it distracted you from the flare of her wide hips and the prominent mound guarding her secrets. She would get me hot one way or another with her last burst of energy then lay back, doze off, and I would begin, baking in a pre-heated oven.

   It wasn't until later I chanced upon the fantasy literature of sleeping beauties. Until then, I thought I was <u>the</u> luckiest man in history to have her complete surrender. Some part of me had desired long hours with a subdued female, one not broadcasting her signal to refocus mine. I'd nuzzle around her breasts, sometimes pulling the nipple between my tongue and sheathed teeth. I'd part her legs, front or back, and let my finger introduce itself inside her, bit by tiny bit, her pussy shifting of its own accord, stimulated to do so by her unconscious nature.

   I'd rub my cock with one hand and use the fingers of my other hand to spread her open so I could look at her intimately, curious to understand how this worked. She would glisten with juice, she seemed to will herself to sleep through it, and I could tell her "mind" wasn't involved even if her butt hole puckered when I stroked it with my thumb. She would change positions so that I got to know every inch of her. I was alone with her body; her mind was shut down.

I wished I could have let her do the same to me but I'd have to be passed-out dead drunk stoned and seriously over-medicated not to wake up to sexual handling.

It was the trust between us that I remember. She wasn't shy about her body, or her feelings for me. She liked having a boyfriend like me, who brought his own desires to bear, one who could be trusted to know her body without taxing her mind. Ohh, that's one image I have not forgotten. I've applied it to other lovers but always in homage to the one who let me see the absolute peace within the female. Defenses down. Powerful drive to endure.

[I was glad when they revealed "morphing" in music videos and movies because my mind had been doing that sort of melding-features since I put together my first fantasy babe and even more so when I had the serene face of my sleeping sweetheart. I saw many imagines flicker across her empty frame. A Sophia Loren build with an Elizabeth Taylor face and a Pat Benatar verve. Eventually, I had real faces and frames and personalities to blend into my fancy.]

There came a day a girl said to me, "I'm pregnant." I'd only known her about a month and we hadn't really done that much sex-wise because she'd had the flu… but we had done enough to scare me. We went to the clinic together and confirmed she was pregnant, about eight weeks. She started to cry, I think she knew it all along, deep in her heart. Not consciously. I helped her move back to her home town and I met her parents. It looked like a good situation for her, they seemed to know who the father was but his name wasn't mentioned to me. Even knowing I wasn't responsible, I felt the pull of new life and was moved by the idea that a real baby was really on the way.

It could have been me. I could be a Dad. Think about that. More than once. Keep thinking.

I'm not one now, but I would learn if duty called. In the interim I am very careful.

↗ ⬇ ↘

In my pursuit of staying stoned, I did business with a variety of other stoners. It seemed to me they were akin to florists or vegetable vendors and, except for the illegal nature of their cargo, I found them rather ordinary. They didn't "make" their pot but they took credit for it, they couldn't force the chemistry yet could coax better plants if aided by luck – or they cultivated a better dealer. I didn't like to argue over weight, I figured the price was arbitrary in the first place since pot lacks a "gold standard" that sets a value to every molecule let alone comparative values for flake and bud. Instead, I insisted on buying a set dollars' worth: I'd buy $50 or $800 or $175 no matter the prevailing #@$ and if the volume matched the money in my eye, the deal was done.

I was not impressed by the elaborate scales of some dealers I knew, they could have weighed an eyelash. In rituals that made me think of ancient spice dealers, after setting the tare weight of the bag, they would add a pinch, throw in a judicious shake, tip-tap the counterweights calibrated to their own exactness. Whatever. When the stuff went in the bag I hefted it in my hand, felt it between my fingers, inhaled deeply, and decided.

My least favorite dealers seemed to rise from a common mist of half-baked notions, there's no polite way to divert a committed idea-freak… especially if they stand between you and your heart's desire like that prickly brick you're buying. Starry-eyed with the grandeur of their own thoughts, I'd be paralyzed into listening to them, enduring lectures on astrology, astronomy, astrophysics, astral projection (and that's just the

Ast… topics). It was as if you paid for access to pot by pretending they made sense. Ah ha. Hmmmm. Um-huh.

I just wanted the dope, I had plenty of my own ideas.

↗ ⬇ ↘

"Oh, no, you put this one on me, not in me."
"I can do that."
"Yes, you can. This is the most fun I've had all year."
"Really, LaLinda? This vibrating knob?"
"Well, it *is* early in the year…"

LaLinda liked sexual stimulation that didn't involve penetration as much as she liked the kind that did. It might have bothered me with somebody else ("wasn't I enough?") but I knew that confidential detail about LaLinda before we were physically intimate. I'd heard her lament other men's tight-minded reaction so I knew to examine my own before expressing it. I had some presumptions that the vagina existed for the purpose of penetration by a penis (preferably mine), I reminded myself of the expanse of female genital tissue that wasn't vaginal and I got the message. I never doubted I'd learn to be a good lover, I stayed alert for opportunities to hear the female side. LaLinda had been trusting me, her chum, with information not offered to her lovers, she and I had reached an instant accord about our suitability as friends and only later crossed the divide to nakedness.

"I can't decide whether to throw my legs open so you can motor all around my crotch or to close my legs tight to trap that magic knob against my mound."
"Then spread, LaLinda, open up to me."
"I want you to watch this."
"I am. Frame your pussy with those lovely thighs."
"I want you to see this."
"I can. Show me you bare naked."
"I want you to mount me."

Kathleen K.

"Not yet, LaLinda… not quite yet."

◁ ⇩ ◁

Having LaLinda as a lover prepared me for all the rest of the loves of my life, I made so many mistakes with her that I knew not to do again. I had to learn that women were <u>women</u> and were different than mothers and sisters and female figures in authority. There is a social minefield around feminist rights and female rites. I couldn't imagine the kind of relationship my grandparents had, where my grandmother did everything for my grandfather, nor even one where my parents reciprocated chores (he went to a day job, did big chores like painting and yard maintenance; she did the relentless indoor duties and social obligations for house and kids).

There was no way for me to contemplate the sexual union of these people I knew, I had to look to less personal examples in films, books, and in my local world. I wanted hot physical relationships, the body element was high on my list, I (thought I) liked blond and lean and broad shouldered. Then I experienced a supple plump brunette, a frail blue-eyed redhead… mostly, I liked fit and female. I was hot to trot, it was like being given a tuned-up sports car when I had my mid-twenties body. It was limber and flush with energy. I could sleep in a bag, dance on rocks, belly-flop down a snowy hill. I may have been emotionally unfinished but my body was solid and reliable. I was not spectacular and I sought lovers who enjoyed the same ordinary health and available status just because it made things easier on all of us to keep track of things. Health + youth = potential.

In the matter of LaLinda, I had my first age-related crisis when I slipped from 32" jeans to 34" because she noticed the tag on my back pocket and teased me about the spread. I'd never really paid attention before because I was living in a fog of youth-induced oblivion but I had <u>always</u> gotten a certain waist size… that was <u>my</u> size. My body had slipped out from under me and I hadn't even realized it! I preferred to think it was prime meat put on by good living but lurking deeper was the sobering thought: I'm getting older.

I hadn't had a crisis this specifically-personal since I sprouted pubic hair. My reaction to *that* had been one of sublime conviction I was a man. I AM MAN. MAN I AM. I looked at my stiffy in the morning, assessing the overnight growth of my shadow. In my own mind, I was equal to any father of ten. When I realized the pant-size change crossed another palpable dividing line between a young man and a new man then a real man I was depressed and elated and queasy. How could it be going by so quickly? I'd had sublime moments and expected more… LaLinda was hot with me and it reinforced my belief that good physical connection was going to underlie my important relationships.

I wanted a woman who could fit in my lap but with enough body weight to push back and fuck me. I liked a meaty-assed lover because I could bury my fingers in the flesh of her butt and direct her vagina to pleasure us both. Breasts weren't a big issue for me, I was a nipple man. It seemed that sucking tit completed a circuit, it was psychically pleasant to be doing it and evidently pleasant to have done. I especially liked it if we twined our legs together so I could press my cock against her highest thigh. We don't talk enough about skin when we discuss sex. With few exceptions, the skin of the women I have known is a tactile pleasure, of a finer grade than my own. I thought my hands were too rough for their satiny surfaces, how dare I touch them at all?

It was LaLinda who brought it all together: body, mind, soul. I wouldn't be guilty of using a woman in the future because that was a waste of all our time.

"Listen to me, baby."

"No. I don't want to be the baby today."

"What do want to be?"

"You be the baby, you lay back, you get rubbed, you get powdered."

"I thought you'd never ask."

"You let go this time, *baby*, you relax your sexual guard and simplify your reactions. That's what you tell me to do, *baby*."

"Ahhh. Preachin' to the preacher."

"Babying a man."

"I'm a strong man, I'm a peaceful man, I'm an accepting man, I'm a willing man. I am a passionate man."

"Shhh, be a quiet man."

I was face down on a beach towel in the middle of a large bed, straddled by a woman massaging oil into my shoulders, my back, my butt, my thighs, my calves, my feet. My front would be next.

I could imagine the timeless touch in what we did, somebody rubbed Nero like this, somebody rubbed the baby Jesus like this, somebody rubbed Hitler, Madame Curie, Martin Luther King, Jr., Bonnie, and Clyde… how many rich ideas had circled the planet while hands touched, how many clear moments? I was blasted into the idea of humanity and was glad I wasn't speaking of these things to the person who was smoothing me because these ideas were too sentimental. How many people had, like me, thought life was forever? How could we lose ourselves in the casing and never know the inner drives?

On another plane of sensation, I was soothed by the pressure of another person on my being, I felt very connected and wanted to experience the sensual grace of surrendering to my surface, letting my body exist in and of itself to be cared for. There was no shyness, no coyness, "I" was not in my own way at the moment.

I could be at ease, I was in good shape, there was confidence. I knew my partner liked me. I felt I could loll under her treatment, uninhibited.

She used two hands on my cock and although it rose it didn't gather any tension, it was engorged, it was warm, but it was not plugged in. My own nipples stood up for much the same reason, nerves.

My partner those nights was quite the little actress, we had many scenes. She wasn't going to be around long, she wouldn't have stayed even if I asked. I'd known her too long, seen her do this too often, to mess with the cycle. She'd pair off for a few months and then drift away. I prepared myself by not missing a single detail as it happened. I could see her and smell her and feel her and hear her every aspect. How rich I could make it. (I wouldn't have to sustain it.) ((I wouldn't get to sustain it.))

Underneath the nanny's skirt I'd find the same flaring backside that lurked in a doctor's smock. Round flat breasts were best seen from below, dangling and swaying with hidden weight. I think of her when I thumb a woman's nipple inward, she asked me to do it and that was a revelation... I'd been rubbing, licking, sucking, pulling; not the oddly delicious (I found) sensation of feeling the inversion, the resistance/ acceptance (hint: it is a poking with the index finger and a flattening when done with the thumb).

I found I liked the staged sex, it was easy to slip into character since they all led to carnal knowledge. I could imagine being a prince offering comfort to a princess or maid; I could believe she was a hot cheerleader when she did the splits in my kitchen. I was realizing how people have to refresh themselves in sex, what it means to lose touch with your truest feelings and settle for mechanics. By assessing the pitfalls, I avoided most of them.

I could be tended to by the kindest hands, I could be raised from my solitary self into communion with another. In the fullest sense, I could share my physical being. I could be in pursuit of a prime drive while achieving sublime expansion of my highest (deepest) self.

Kathleen K.

I finally figured out a standard cash box was the best place for my everyday pot, the upper coin-and-bill area had handy spaces for papers, clips, tiny jars of hash and a porta-pipe. This all-purpose top could be lifted out to reveal space for a most excellent tray holding my current supply underneath, nestled baggies of front-line stash. The raised-edge tray I found to fit on the bottom of the box was convenient for rolling, it had a high gloss finish so pot didn't stick to it, it had a shallow end for holding papers. I would roll about a half dozen joints at a time... well-balanced, good smokers (no sidewinding, although I remember realizing since heat rises you should turn the unburnt side up and take a deep hit; unless the j is fatally flawed, the coal should even itself again) (watch for falling embers, they make those distinctive round holes in your clothes). Manicure scissors are excellent for trimming roach ends. When a joint stops drawing, pinch off the wet end to open air flow. Keep the roach dry and alive by putting it between your fingers but not all the way through, then put your lips on your fingers.

I had the distinction of being able to roll joints one-handed which I perfected one long-ago summer in the back of a van full of weedies like myself. We crossed through fourteen states, back and forth to rock concerts, rearranging our relationships along the way. We were the prototype for those reality-TV shows throwing a half-dozen young people together except we didn't get the cool apartment. Passions mellowed with the pot, we bumped along the highways and by-ways having firsthand experience with people along the way, not really noticing that even in one summer we all grew older. We got ripped off once at a three-day concert, only luck led us to the perpetrator. I saw a guy wearing one of our shirts and backed him up against a tree. He was so stoned it made me dizzy to talk to him. I led him back to his "camp" and then sent a nearby kid running over to the van to fetch some of my friends. We were scrupulous to take back only our own things although the guy had collected a righteous pile of other people's belongings. I didn't care to listen to his rambling insights into the emptiness of ownership so I had him sit down and study the sky for a while. After that, somebody had to stay at our van, and guard rotation became a point of argument. It pitted realism against our wish to float in a sea of love. Even in <u>that</u> sea, it turned out we prized our own stocked raft.

⥽ ⬇ ⬲

"I'm telling you, in the old days they rubbed the plants in their hands then scraped off the resin. That's how you make hashish."

"All I know is you get it from the mama plant, but I don't think rubbing the hell out of the stuff in this baggie is going to turn it into hash."

"This shit's all dried out. Hash is from the fresh bud, the wet bud… the rich bud. It's the essence. Smoke-grade dope is what's left over."

"I think it's opposite, hash is from the stalks and the trim."

"That's doesn't sound right."

"It is, though. It's all about the resin in the stalk. That's the science, bud. Or should I say 'bud science'."

⥽ ⬇ ⬲

Knowing drugs were illegal, I never made it a habit to keep my stuff out in easy reach. It was not worth getting busted for, and it also presented too great a temptation to some of my visitors. I was quick to share but I had a sense of my stock and was always disappointed when I realized somebody had dipped in without asking. Think about it, you are stealing something you crave from somebody who must want the same stuff or they wouldn't have it. This isn't like being hungry and boosting food (from a mega-chain, if you must)… stealing pot in a fellow toker's home is a breach of bond. Hiding your action is a sign of guilt.

The cash box was a portable solution, it had a handle on top, it locked. It certainly would have attracted a burglar since it obviously held something prized but what could I do? Nail it down? I keep my deep stash in the bank (I find Tupperware® very effective for everyday use but for safety deposit everything is first dried and pressed in foil, shrink-wrapped in a heat-sealed baggie then put in a heavy paper envelope with the provenance noted). They look like well-wrapped books or rectangular art. I go in every once in a while and rearrange the contents. I stash backup pot, releasing older items to be rotated into the active supply and pull out goodies as needed. Sometimes I didn't have much there but always I keep backup. If something special came through town, I was careful to set some aside. If I die, the box designee is LaLinda, who can claim innocence as to its contents if challenged. She never once went to the bank with me although she did know exactly where it was.

◊ ⇩ ◊

LaLinda never lost her taste for bud and over the years we have explored much territory while we clouded up. The time was companionable, we were both willing to surrender a few hours to our "pot'n _____" evenings. We had pot'n movies, pot'n long walks, pot'n yard work, pot'n more pot.

◊ ⇩ ◊

Brenda wore gloves when she handled me, sometimes lace gloves for a strange touch, or latex gloves that I soon associated with being fingered up the ass. In some ways, Brenda wasn't my type, she didn't like to talk much, she preferred loud music. Overcoming my initial disinclination toward her, I was rewarded by a fertile experience. I had never been handled so thoroughly as Brenda did with her gloved hands, and I understood that she was partly a sex-machine, doing for me what she sensed that I wanted, releasing energies I didn't (usually) admit were there, she pulled me forward from one step back (one layer sheathed). I tensed when she spanned my crack, I had a flash of my own exact position right before I myself dropped an index finger onto someone else's puckered hole. Tap, tap, Brenda was there (there!) but it wasn't <u>really</u> Brenda, it was the glove touching me, she couldn't really _feel_ me, I was not completely exposed, latex is precisely impersonal. We all know the exposure was not physical, she got her cues from my deep breathing as she prodded, simulating the insertion of a cock in a vagina, I couldn't miss the symbolism nor the literally thrilling aspect of being invaded. When I was younger and less experienced, I would have dismissed this as sick and twisted but what did I know then? It still ain't my daily do.

Brenda wore elbow-length white gloves to play with herself, her hands fluttering like doves in the branches of her sex.

For fucking, she liked to be rolled back onto her shoulders, her legs pressed against my chest, her calves hiked up over my shoulders, and I would slip in so deep I found it hard to brace myself sufficiently. I fell in love with the contours of her vagina, it hugged my nuts with thick, wet lips, it rippled with muscle the entire length of my cock. Her juice had no taste but her scent was intoxicating, I must have looked like a cat in a catnip patch. The hotter she got, the better she smelled, she was cooking.

There is no flavor-scale for women's sex fluid, for men you've got the salty element and viscosity but with women there is that _spirituous_ jolt as you immerse yourself in this most intimate sea {texture}.

In Brenda's case, I could catch her scented signal but on my tongue she felt like thick water, clear but possessing weight, it wouldn't splash, it would smear.

The junction of legs and ass in the valley of the vault— I could rapture on the natural cunning of this fertile basin, how it hides yet flowers. I am not ashamed to consider sex physically – how hard it is to explain otherwise. What is it about the legs as they part – they retract to form a frame. Until you've seen more than a few up close and personal, you can't appreciate how different genitals are, and how some don't seem to match with the rest of the person. I have found no formula for predetermining the nature of a woman's genital presentation. Thanks to tight pants you can find the mounded ones, and pre-select the rump or flank. You cannot know the rest, it is her secret, that oneness of hers to grant another. Still hidden after all these hundreds of years of "progress" in education and social engineering... we love our secrets.

It came as some surprise to me how differently "laid out" women were within their gender, and I figured that's why the penis is not rigid when hard (it's hinged), it can be angled through a certain arc to accommodate these inward tiltings and the variation in depth. What a difference an inch makes, some women were deep enough that I could plunge in while others were for dipping, where you concentrate on the opening and do not dive. I've experienced almost painful constriction, when fully dilated was still too tight for me. There is such a need to be tender when your partner is built tight or dry, you can sense when you've reached her capacity.

And how exhilarating if you reach the next level, where a relaxed female allows you to go deeper than your dick, to push in farther than the objective length of your penis, to slam forward-inward-upward until your ass puckers up to shove. Total rightness and the trust to abandon yourself to the *push~me pull~you* of sex, giving and taking through taking and giving.

༺ ⇩ ༻

Ronnie was a talker when she got turned on, her voice dropped an octave and slowed. I picked positions that kept my ear near her lips because she spoke softly about what we were doing together, how it felt to be pried open, why she liked two fingers better than three, how hot my cock felt slipping through her fingers. She had a gift, engaging me on a little-used level, making me think in order to raise the blood into my head, culminating in a more balanced orgasm than the mindless dick-bombs when all it is is a bang.

"Hey, lover man, hey... what's that toy between my legs? Did you know that knob on the end would notch perfectly against my hood? Dirty dog, you wanted me wet like this— it's not too much, is it? Is it too smooth? Too juicy? I don't think so. And neither do you! You like it sloppy hot, rub your cock in it, come on, you know you want to.

"Stick it up in here, honey, where we both know it belongs. You can wiggle in right here, I got a place saved just for you. Give me more of that, that's what I want, to feel you trying. Man like you, he needs his pussy, works hard for the pussy, you know you think that way… this is a reward, it's what you get for being good. Be my good boy, now, show me how good you can be, how sensual, how confident, how hard.

"Here's the secret, baby, the goodness of life, dip yourself into me, deeper and deeper, fall into me, lover, heart and all, make love to me, tender but press-press-*press*ing and <u>*urge*-ent</u> — you fuck me, sweet man, you fuck me now."

Ronnie said she forgot most of what she said during sex, it was something she didn't feel she controlled. It was an aspect of her sexuality she didn't mind discussing with me. She told me other guys didn't always like the soundtrack, one asked her to be quiet because he couldn't keep count (!). Mostly, she knew it spurred guys on, she felt it in the snap of their bodies, she let the words flow. I knew that she liked me and I felt comfortable in this conversation when I asked if she said the same stuff to everybody or was it tailored? She admitted to having some favorite themes, but mostly it flowed, she tried various angles and pursued the ones that agitated her listener. I tried to tell her what it was like to *hear* her thoughts as I took her body and she realized how much freer she felt to move if she distracted (?) herself with the verbal works, she thought silent sex could be grim but we did do it that way from time to time, for the purpose of staying balanced. Ronnie didn't like looking into people's eyes, she said it was too spooky, so we'd be absolutely quiet as we let our bodies make adjustments, suppressing our moans, averting our eyes, using our breath to control the energy flow. Ronnie learned silence wasn't grim at all, it was a different focus enriching on its own terms. We also used her hot tub, something I had not been overly fond of at the beginning of the craze (I thought "bacteria soup"). I wanted tubbing to feel like swimming, tub water was more highly charged than in a pool, hot and close and "on you". Ronnie liked to sit, buoyant, across my lap, I'd slide one arm behind her back and gaze at her dripping breasts, I'd raise one leg to tilt her closer to my belly, we'd kiss (with our eyes closed).

Wet, feeling shiny— skin soaked free of the world, bland, like boiled food, nutritious but not tasty, not personal yet. Ronnie had a tantalizing biochemistry, she never had bad breath, her sweat smelled clean even after a day's work; at the small of her back and behind her knees she exuded a toasty smell. Her sex seeped a memorable mix of hot pine and honey, the aroma subtle, it slid past the usual receptors and registered in some other sense. I could not put a word to it but I can close my eyes and associate that with libation. Ronnie would transfer that scent to her nips, to her throat, when we made love it would rise around her.

"Peel me open, find that seam and separate it slowly. Don't rush, let me feel the night here between my legs, and your breath brushing past these secret lips. Pinch me shut over my clit, gather up my sex skin and cover that button, then press against it, stay distant but get intense. It's wetter now, find the source of that. Yes, you did, didn't you? You are at point zero, the point of no return.

"You smell like me now, you're smudged with me, it's between your fingers, it's on your chin, the more you face me, the more I want you to fuck me, every jab of your tongue is a tease for your prick, this is -- nice. Real nice and real.

"Get your fingers in there, don't make me wait! I'm twisting inside, coiled to take your cock, I am prepared to fuck the holy hell out of you. Lick me out, get me ready, suck me up, get me hotter, then slide on and plunge into me, plunge all the way into me, uncoil in me, you fucker, get yourself where you belong.

"You're built for me, built like a rocket, sleek, you get a great hard on, it's a classic boner. Get in here and get some sex – I got some boxed and ready to go. It's spread here and waiting for you. Give me your dick, come closer and make me really feel it, come on, give it with feeling, push it with pride. You've got a hot cock seeking a target and I've got a wet pussy to aim it at. Come on, angel man, fall for me."

↗ ⬇ ↖

Guys talk about sex, they see strategy and achievement but not growth. I gave up expecting much insight from men in groups, and stumbled over a rare source of male discussion only once in a while. One guy I met for coffee on Tuesday evenings for about a year. We had been asked to share a booth in the over-crowded coffee shop one stormy night and as strangers he and I were able to plow past barriers usually erected to deflect sudden friendships. His wife had tossed him out for the evening so she could have a bridge party. My god, he said, she used to make fun of his mother for that! We got to talking how we were and were not like our own parents which snapped us into a reflective mood. I got a lot of things straightened out in my head by talking freely with Cameron.

Cameron figured as a single guy I was getting lots of sex, just as I blithely thought that regular sex was at least one advantage of marriage. I had been stunned to realize how sex diminished *unless it was worked on* for singles and coupled alike. He and I had been on the same journey but in different ways: his wife was his sole companion in this while I changed partners, he had a long history with her while I had many events. We had learned through time and opportunity to make love to our women.

Cameron once ranted about a ruined afternoon of lovemaking when the bedroom curtains proved too sheer and they exchanged shocked looks with the mail carrier who was cutting across the yard. It put his wife off daylight sex completely. I suggested he take her shopping to get new drapes for the bedroom, toss in a matching quilt for the bed and more pillows. Offer to help her construct a love nest. I'd seen enough of women's talk shows to pick up on one great hint: Do something about the things that bother you (if only deciding not to let them bother you). Invest in your bedroom so it *works* as a retreat; most women understand nesting. Make this your stage, control the lighting, the air, the sounds. It doesn't have to be a Hugh Hefner sex pad, it can be as simple as adding one dimmer switch and buying a navy blue window shade to hang behind the light-permeable drapes you normally prefer.

◊ ⇩ ◊

Cameron used alcohol like I used pot, so it seemed fair that we both abstained during our weekly coffee; we let the caffeine rev us up a bit. We'd have pie and ice cream with our third cup and discuss the purpose of our sex, individually and as members of the male gender.

Cameron's wife wasn't ready to have kids, although she planned to have at least two when the time seemed right – to her. Cameron let her lead on this as long as it was clear he was a family man. He equated reproductivity as the motivator for fidelity and accorded his upcoming fatherhood high status in the marital equation. He wanted to press her on this because he felt a need for some change. They went to work they didn't hate, took great vacations, had sex three times a week, dinner out on Saturdays and Wednesdays; one cultural and one sporting event together each month; to the shore in the spring, to the woods in the autumn. Four "free" days a month for separate chums. He wanted more than this orderly existence, he craved the free-for-all reality of a family with growing children, he watched others and envied the complications of Billy Boy at soccer and Susy Girl at gymnastics, the can't-miss school plays and refrigerator art. He and I agreed that everybody could benefit from refrigerator art: I actually kept one stunning image I bought at a neighborhood school fair, a sheet of letter-sized paper, completely blank, at the center of the bottom edge were three human figures, each about three-quarters of an inch tall, plus horses of the same small scale, done with care by an eight-year old. This had a mesmerizing effect on me, what held my attention was the vastness of the world implied in occupying such a small strip of it at the bottom, but enriching the tiny world with details. Frame of reference.

⟲ ⇩ ⟳

He says: "I tell her I'm not asking for much, just three times a week." She says: "Yeah, it's like he wants it every other day."

⟲ ⇩ ⟳

I had art paper and colored pencils in the employees' room at the store so their kids could submit drawings on store-related topics. If a drawing was used on an in-store poster, the creator got a framed copy and a store credit for their family, in addition they got a cash certificate in their own name. I changed the posters frequently, using part of my advertising budget this way since I doubted newspaper ads were the source of my core revenue. I worked the neighborhood, I developed an interest in community events, I expanded my office supply section and gave a quarter-aisle to auto supplies. I made sure to have good scissors for sale, kitchen gadgets, film, picnic supplies, light bulbs, rope (don't ask me why, but it moves off the shelves quite quickly). I like knowing I've got the ability to make a good store— basically, I'm a super-shopper buying things at a good price so I can pass them on at a fair price. I don't mark up diapers or baby food much, I hit the wine and beer to make up for it (which might, in the long run, account for more diaper sales…).

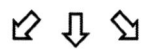

⟲ ⇩ ⟳

Kathleen K.

I don't usually blow a joint in the car, and certainly not in a strange neighborhood, but I had agreed to help grandma-sit a friend's live-in relative for four days while they went on a cruise. The old lady, Grace, was losing her mind and filling up the empty spaces with foul racist images, she was on the waiting list for her church's nursing home although they blanched when she visited there. She had a pleasant voice and clear expression on her face as she described the mailman donging the neighborhood dogs and the Chinee whore up the street pretending to run a laundry so men could take off their underpants behind the counter and she'd clean their behinds with her face. I got my own three hours of "respite care" from a paid nurse each day and I dashed to my vehicle, my privacy, my silence, and even that didn't wash her away, she'd been a music teacher, raised a fine family, now she estimated penis size of "bucks" on TV. (She never slept.)

I drove around their section of town, getting used to the traffic flow, then picked a quiet neighborhood to slide through; kids were at school, folks were at work. I don't excuse lighting the joint in the car, it was crazy-stupid, but what can I say? I'd been horrified listening to Grace's world view after one day. My friend and her husband must have needed Thorazine to function.

I looked to the left as a car pulled up next to me at the intersection and it was a cop, he looked me over, noticed the doobie in my hand and shot his eyes back to my face. What could I do? I shut my mouth and nodded my head, crumbling the joint out the window so he could see it was destroyed. He deliberately looked at his watch, narrowed his eyes and shook his head at me. This was bad! I was saved because it was lunch time. He bleeped his siren at me just to see me jump then he wheeled left and drove away.

That is the absolute closest I've felt to being busted. And I didn't care. If Grace's fate lay at the end of the rainbow, I wanted to reconsider my long-range plans. It was a stroke that re-wired some of her circuits, she wasn't a whole person any more, her linkage slipped and she wandered around verbalizing reptilian thoughts.

Busted! I'd feared it so often I grew bored with the idea. As my life solidified, I knew I'd have one golden chance to "go into treatment" for my anti-social behavior. I looked good on paper. Domiciled. Employed. Solvent. Rational. As long as I didn't traffic except for personal use I was under the DEA radar. My value as a snitch wasn't even a complete rung up the distribution ladder as my current "dealer" was a househusband who got his own pot free by middling $100 transactions. His wife would let him smoke if it didn't cost them any money and if she didn't have to see it, smell it or hear about it.

It's hard to be considered an outlaw over such mild consequences. Don't give me the stepping-stone-to-heroin argument (gateway drug). I don't buy it. Having a beer doesn't lead to Skid Row for everybody, not even for the majority. Drug classifications are a bureaucratic thing, misplacing marijuana near heroin rather than nicotine, at the same time allowing alcohol to flow through society with disastrous impact. Don't get me going on use and abuse of prescription psychopharmacology. Either ban it all or allow it all, but the hypocrisy blunts any attempt to resolve the questions of "pursuit of happiness" and "right to privacy".

I valued my privilege to associate with whom I selected, to worship life as I saw fit, to speak of my beliefs openly— simple freedoms of a fully functioning citizen of the United States. I knew my leaders made mistakes, I read about them daily, I knew they didn't have particular insight into the human condition when it came to sex, drugs, rock and roll, or military might. They were wrong about pot and it made this element of my life inconvenient but not impossible. If you think about it, it's a chummy distribution system at my level.

The movie "Midnight Express" killed any fantasy I had of dealing as a way to avoid working. Working was easier than jail. Work was only $1/3^{rd}$ of $5/7^{th}$ of the week, jail was 100% of the time.

Kathleen K.

Now I lay me down to sleep... another pleasure in my life. I keep the bed in good condition, flipping the mattress, replacing it routinely, buying high quality sheets often, having them washed with delicate soap in hot water, running a second cycle without soap on high agitation. My grandmother taught me that women inspect your sheets as a measure of your worthiness (shoes too). I bought an oversized bedside table so I could have a lamp, a pot repository for roaches and clips that acted as a cover for a small ashtray, some matches and a lighter, a book or two, a notebook for writing, two identical pens, a phone with ring light. I had a lapdesk (basically a beanbag bottom with a 12×15" plastic "desktop"). Handier than hell to hold a notebook because it settled on your legs. I don't eat in bed – I have a chair and table for that in my bedroom, it seats two for intimate snacking.

I like that the bed is big enough to share, I didn't get a king size because it isn't necessary and so the queen size it is. [Can't they just call them small (twin), medium (full/double), large (queen), extra large (king)?] At any rate, that size bed can be cozy in my room and still allow two life-sized humans to sleep in comfort. I love to have a warm bum to press against in the night but I don't like breath in my ear or sleeping straight like a stick. I cuddle when I'm conscious and can appreciate it.

My idea of morning sex is to wake up, wash face, brush teeth, comb hair, have coffee, get naked, hump like monkeys. I'm not a big fan of rubbing my sleepy face on somebody. Coffee is required because I'd like to be able to remember what happens. Morning sex differs from night sex in my mind. I've figured out how to darken my room when I want to "cave" but some mornings I want the windows open, the air on my skin (where it isn't pressed to other skin).

In the light of day, lovemaking is clearer and more subtly shaded, sun doing what light bulbs cannot, dappled sunshine is not flickering candle light, nothing looks the same. Even closing your eyes communicates the fact of day light behind your lids. Sex is associated with bed time, especially by young children, they see it as complicated hugging in the dark and this strong feeling is reinforced by a society that puts erotic education under the covers. Day time sex is perversely indulgent, as if there were "better" things to do after sun up.

↖ ⬇ ↘

I watch the widowers at the store, if they shopped before their wives died, it was most often with a list written by their wife. Alone, they continue to buy the same kinds of food for a while then begin to shift, an item at a time, toward food of their own choosing. Many are drawn to the balance of the modern frozen meal, it's meat-vegetable-starch on a plastic platter... for lunch, especially. It's important to me that I acknowledge all the "novice" homemakers, so I stock pot holders and dish towels and a few tablecloths near the kitchen gadgets. I remember trying to make my own place livable, when I began to cook and then to clean as a grown-ass man. Party-time was over. I needed a pail, a mop, some floor goop remover.

I still partied but it was no longer a lifestyle.

I'd go to a party to score some bud (if I could) then return to my work-a-day world, looking forward to my evening stones.

I <u>am</u> a natural stoner, I find the effects of marijuana fit perfectly into my moods. I might get high and take a brisk walk, befuddled with thought, cruising over bumpy ground (mentally and physically), stretching into the future for answers inside myself. I could make connections this way, see that I over-reacted to one situation because it rang of another. I enjoy thinking with different parts of my brain and there is a huge difference between watching *Now, Voyager* and walk-run-walking for forty-four minutes. I could be stoned on each occasion but it felt different every time.

There is the same smoothness as that of a well-timed drink, like Valium to some, the cushion between "out there" and "in here" that seemed the point of focus. I could lead myself with music, often planning hours ahead as if knowing where I'd want to go later. I could listen to Carol

King and feel part of my youth surge forward, when it was possible to be totally baked, fried, yet safe and even sound. I'd hit my aria CD and feel passionate yearnings for love, ageless undying love I'd want to sing out. If I want to work on anger stuff, I hit snarly rock, strut rock, back-off rock, I'm-too-hot-for-you rock.

I can meditate to Gregorian chants when I'm stoned, tuning into the many voices in the choir, not so much for the catholic nature but for the precision of those individual people unified, soaring, dipping, landing in unison on a series of single notes. Pot is a layer of gauze so the world can be contained while I roam inside myself.

I spend the majority of my hours straight so I'm very aware how unstoned I am after I come down. I don't have hangovers from pot, I don't lose weekends at a time, I see my drinking friends physically suffering from their alcohol use. They dehydrate and leach vitamins from themselves, getting drunk is what they do, it isn't like they get a booze buzz on and go running or meditate. Whether it's in the downtown tavern or the uptown study, drinking is visibly tough on the body over time.

The "person-ality" exerts itself over both genders, you get tidy men and aggressive women, there isn't only one way to be male or female (a person). I wondered at all those guys who felt being guys gave them the right to seize, to frighten and coerce. My manliness seems to find that violence shortsighted. In my natural desire to spread my seed, I make sure I pick quality recipients of sound judgment. Sexy to me means strong, sure, straightforward. A female who can't protect herself would not be my candidate to take on the job of breeding my legacy. So much of human nature is keyed to reproductivity -- and the prevention of it— that I have considered carefully what I believe about sexual attraction.

Appearance. Not a specific appearance but a woman's overall appearance, or presentation, of herself. How does she stand, what does she wear? Tottering at me on high heels is a turn off (impractical) but striding by wearing a fitted sharp-heeled boot is a turn on. I like to see a woman braless in a long sleeved white shirt tucked into a flattering pair of Levi's. I like one-piece bathing suits cut high on the thigh and low under the arms (showing the side-swell of her breasts). I prefer she wear a long loose skirt on our picnics, bare bottomed.

    I used to go parking with this one woman (we were in our late 20's) because she liked to expose her ta-tas while I fingered her, she'd milk my dick at the same time; we *loved* it. She would wear loose shorts so our hands could move freely between her legs, I liked seeing her breasts in a bra at first, eventually she'd bare herself. Her head would fall to the side as if listening to a far off voice. Her nipples would pucker and my cock would firm. This was safe sex for us, biochemically and emotionally, there was no clutching, no twining, we shared energies more commonly released alone. We liked to be with each other when we came and that was so complete we quickly recovered and returned to our real lives. I found her style attractive even as we both knew nothing really existed between us, we weren't going to be making any love. It was exciting and friendly, she considered it a skirting of the edge of her self-imposed celibacy. She remembered to pace herself, to tune in to my state, and I did my best to vary my responses so we were thoroughly stimulated before we bumped it up the final notch.

    She had clitoral orgasms, her fingers never slipped inside, at most she'd coax her wetness forward. She would put her index and ring fingers alongside the pussy lips and pull them together then curve her middle finger against that fold and rub herself. She talked of a dildo she used at home when she had reason to exercise herself in that way… she preferred a medium sized cock with a definite head.

    Her hand jobs were great, she was especially good at arousing me as she moved her hand up, over and around my dick. I'd have to say she had a superior technique in that she encircled and enfolded the head in imaginative ways so I felt that welcome pressure of being surrounded, grasped (accepted). She also used the fabric of my loose runner's shorts to stimulate my sexual hunger. She knew my desires perfectly and I would fantasize about really doing it with her, letting ourselves couple.

She admitted to similar thoughts which intensified them, of course. We had agreed one hand each, over the gear-shift, no torso leaning, no face. It was an interlude for us and as such I found it stupendous. She finally broke away from these meetings, she considered our time together a success and she had, indeed, hooked back into the idea of having a sex partner. I purely enjoyed the mirror-sex with a bright, capable person. She didn't like to finger her vagina and I was the exact opposite. Symbiosis.

As I learned to navigate the sensitive parts of the female anatomy, I grew in appreciation of their variety, proverbial snowflakes (none alike, all with sharp edges that melt away with body heat). I am drawn to a pronounced mound, a plump straight seam rather than fluted, a deep hood. I react most strongly. In all ways, women are hardwired to response zones in me. I am more attracted to a mannish female than a feminized male. I'm curious about different cocks only in the sense of their bio-actuality: how they feel in women. Being shy of marriage, I got my share of Lonely Uncle jokes but that worry, at least, was spared me. I enjoyed women as an endless wonder.

Besides, who would believe plain old me was having such a good time? I seemed quiet, I had a day job, saw my family every holiday. Just, some nights I'd be in a steamy car getting shot off like a cannon as my passenger gushed alongside me. Maybe everybody else is out, like me, on their secret missions. I don't think so. But I don't know.

One night, I found a single Polaroid picture stuck in one of my old sports-gear bags. I had used that bag for "spontaneous" nights out when I wanted a few condoms, some lube, a spare joint, fresh underwear and socks, a small towel, travel size shampoo, you know— whatever. In silhouette I saw pictured a woman I'll call Alyce bent forward at the waist, her breasts hanging down free, the shape-shadow of a dildo protruded at the back about four inches. I remembered the dildo was a milky brown against her olive thighs, and I noticed that my suck marks didn't show in the picture but they were there, I remember that.

She had always had the fantasy of being an exhibitionist but no opportunity presented itself. She blurted this thought out one night when I was going down on her, and the raw emotion in her voice convinced me I'd have to work on arranging that. She had a deep chest and broad ass, she'd be putting a lot of skin in the air if she bared herself completely. I'd suggested she might want to try it with an audience of one first. Alyce thought perhaps we could go out to a state park and find a quiet campsite. There was only a remote possibility of being stumbled upon in the short period she would stand nude, we agreed to do this. She wore a long black dress that zipped far down the back, she shrugged it forward until her breasts were free, and then showed her belly, her navel, her crotch. She stood there, still, for almost five minutes, it *was* a lot of flesh in the air, she glowed warm in the dawn light, and then presented me with a gift-wrapped package in which lay an extra long dildo. I figured out that even fully thrust inside of her, a large portion would hang out and that turned me on. We got high and took our time inserting the toy to its maximum tolerance, taking a few quick photos. I didn't realize at the time that I'd ever see another one of those pictures again. (She must have slipped it there when I wasn't looking because I faithfully tossed the pictures on the campfire as we had agreed.)

Alyce was dynamite, packed tight inside her self, rightfully fearful of live detonator males. I was given to understand that our relationship would be intense but not permanent. I could live with that. I had no interest in an everlasting relationship with her but the thought of getting my hands on her voluptuous body was reason enough to accept a short-term association. I would cherish her, fill her, soak myself in her, enacting the deepest of all human exchanges: bodies knowingly given.

Toking dope together was out of the question, Alyce was in law enforcement and she feared even contact smoke could show on a drug test. She didn't care that I smoked when she wasn't around, we'd known each other long before she got her badge so I didn't worry she would bust me at this late date. In some ways, doing her straight gave me a chance to enjoy myself differently. It wasn't coincidence that she wanted to break a taboo by exposing herself: I saw her living within the lines at work, enforcing rules for the common good. Noble and all that, but, she says, after all, a girl's got to live!

I did miss the point of convergence I would have experienced when my high established itself... I'd forged a strong association between pot and sex. Times spent with Alyce were amiable, we considered each other as lucky to "be ourselves" and pursue affectionate contact. I used to wonder why I was willing to accept oddly-limited relations with various women but it seemed at the time I had a chance to connect with the private forces in a woman's life when I let her set the structure. Had I insisted on all or nothing, I'd have had a lot less sex but also a lot less fun between the sex. Daring to offer myself was all I could do, the rest was up to each woman in our particular situation.

Timing was important, I had my best luck with women who were assessing themselves, preparing for a transition in their lives, curious about the untested passions. I was a suitable physical specimen and— most importantly— stable. My kind of female doesn't gravitate to greedy, needy men. I was flattered they accepted me knowing how many men could have served them and I was bemused that so many men wouldn't know how to tap into such trust.

Listen. Watch. Learn. Share.

Don't be their girl friend, swapping gossip. Don't try to drive the deal, pressure forces the woman to adopt a defensive pose. Relax and let her observe you in action. Understand you want an intelligent assessment so as to be selected for the right reasons. Simple male moved to honor the utterly immense sexuality welling inside the female. She's the lock AND the key.

Alyce transferred out to Boston, I hear from her every Christmas, erotic holiday greeting cards with just her signature. Explicit pen-and-ink line drawings of humans in contact, the equivalent of pairs ice skating, ancient body language— the bend toward, the handing off, the enfolding, the spins. Each card was an original, and I'd ponder the fourteen lines that made a kneeling person astride a prone person for that year's pose.

She explained she'd do the same drawing for each card, free hand, some quick, some slow, signing each one and addressing its envelope so the art was part of the bigger process of contemplating the recipient's name, their address (how were things in… San Diego… Calgary… Florence?).

All this from a Polaroid.

↗ ⇓ ↘

Drinking just ain't for me. I went down that path a ways, and must say the neighborhood tavern provided me some wonderful evenings. At first, you think you're drawn to the people but eventually you realize it's the fog you like, drunk is drunk varying only in degree. I was a different "me" with a few beers in me, plus I was emboldened by the others' inebriation. Besides, it says something when you meet a person in a tavern: it isn't church, it isn't work, it isn't home.

I got sponsored into one tavern's in-crowd by a lady I knew. She lived alone in a tall skinny house about three blocks from the bar. I learned this location was critical to her plan to avoid a second DUI. She intended to be *impaired* when she left the neighborhood bar (about 11:15 p.m.), that was the point of her drinking after all. She wanted to get convivial, boozy, but leave before the mood turned at midnight. She didn't pay attention to the road when in that frame of mind and, since she wasn't going to quit drinking any time soon, she found a way to drink and not drive. We'd stroll the short distance home, still jazzed by the interaction down at the tavern, old enough to know how to attain and maintain intoxication.

Donna and I made a good pair, she had a wry and biting wit that kept me on my mental toes. She was tart without being bitter. She had yellow hair and royal blue eyes that turned black in the moonlight. I thought of Nordic maidens when I became familiar with her body. Her shoulders and hips were in proportion with a long sturdy torso between them. Her skin was the color of sunshine on a white rose, glowing with the feel of pink. She liked to burrow against my body wearing only a bra and panties, me confined only by my underwear. Tactile stimulation, her rounded

Kathleen K.

thighs resting against my leaner ones, the scent of her neck distinct from the ever-clean smell of her hair.

Donna didn't get naked with the lights on. Period. She had to gentle herself down when in the maddening grasp of the male. It flipped switches in her so we learned to let the agitation drain away. She explained to me how often men rejected her because they didn't want to wait until she relaxed. Unlike me, they failed to sustain the arousing sensation of body contact without advancing their own agenda. I'd while away the time thinking sensuous thoughts and suppressing my own impetuous sexuality to reach for a deeper, more mystical approach. She was slow to warm but then she held her heat.

She had installed one of those clapper switches on her love lamp, the specific light she kept on so she wouldn't get naked until she was good and ready. It cast a flattering light on us both, just enough illumination to see her nipples thicken against the fabric of her bra. She especially liked to touch my cock while I was still wearing my underwear. It made me feel anonymously explored, palpitated. Donna was assessing strength and flexibility, the weight and length of me. She was dull-minded from the liquor wearing off and half-lulled to sleep by our quiet cuddling, she slipped into a sexual mood like a drip gathers itself to drop.

Her lovemaking style was passive, she placed herself in my hands. I'd learned to tell her when to move, and she always did when I told her to, but she didn't move if I didn't say so. She had told me about her first husband's teasing her overeager humping but it was so long ago she couldn't remember if he was right about that. She didn't want to know. Her pleasant acceptance of our shared sensations kept our lovemaking from becoming passionate. She was grieving her second husband, a man rendered impotent by advanced diabetes, a suicide (by morphine overdose) ((no one ever admitted to supplying him the needle, the drugs, but I was convinced Donna hadn't done so, I came to believe it was his brother who thought it was love to let him go)). To capitalize on the tender side of their marital love but diminish the frustration she remained in her panties and bra with him when they slept together. He said he couldn't bear to see her naked, it would be a feast set in front of a man with his teeth wired

93/131

shut. In the dark he could pet her to orgasm, in the dark he could liberate her breasts; still, even in the dark, he could be overcome by a lack of physical fulfillment that broke both their hearts. No kick. All these years later, she didn't give her nakedness to me because it had been denied to her true lover.

The tavern Donna and I frequented served unsalted peanuts and low salt pretzels, the eating was not to stimulate your thirst (the comraderie did that). It is congenial to snack from a shallow bowl of simple food chased by cold beer. It was the bar's habit to order food in about eight o'clock, we rotated through Italian, Chinese, Deli, Fish'n Chips that we ate family style. The bartender got free eats for organizing the order.

It was important to Donna that "her tavern" was not dark and hopeless, it wasn't filled with sodden drunks smelling vaguely of piss (perhaps because it dribbled on their shoe tops). This place entertained people who played pool, or cards, they provided music for the sound system and would play guest selections if the majority didn't object. The newspaper was pulled out, and far-reaching discussions ensued. They always hoisted one after reading first the births, then the weddings, finally the obituaries, out loud.

Donna had never slept with one of the guys from the tavern, it would have changed her whole "sister" dynamic. She didn't want to reveal herself to any specific one of them, it was important to her that her man be seen as an import, with no history of his own with these people. In the first place, she and I could agree to presenting a certain face of our relationship, it appeared to others that I was in pursuit of her while the fact was I'd been drawn into the situation by Donna's invitation. I played the woo-er, the beau, so that she could tease me for the benefit of our crowd. A drinking crowd.

After a few hours visiting with them, the edges of the room disappeared and all the action seemed to center around our tables. We'd have a double-solitaire game crowding out the beer mugs on one table, at another the ashtray might be filled with bottle tops we were saving to flip against the curb later. (The various twists and warps of the cap added a high degree of difficulty -- they weren't uniform like pennies for pitching.)

Kathleen K.

Donna would sit with one leg thrown over mine, or her hand on my thigh, physically connected with me in a proprietary way; our relationship served some purpose in the group, lent her substance as an individual by being the member of a pair. I was loyal and true to her, it would have been a sacrilege to eye other women when we were in our little world.

I was smoking dope on my own, she didn't mix pot with beer. Once in a while somebody would bring in a joint and I'd step outside to take a few tokes to be sociable but then it wasn't really like getting stoned all the way, it was a head-topper. In a sense, I was appreciated for "being myself" when I wasn't being me at all. I was playing the role of Donna's man friend.

Donna was more the pill type than I expected, she loved to slip into a downer drowse, timing herself to get home before the serious lassitude struck her limbs. It wasn't my kind of high (low) to share but I didn't mind her enjoying herself in this way. She'd be too out of it to really take care of herself, I'd have to guide her to the bathroom and wait outside the door calling out reminders of what to do next; once I piloted her back to bed I'd solemnly explain what I hoped to achieve sexually and she'd nod along earnestly but then she forget and seemed surprised – every time – when my hand slid between her legs.

Even relaxed to a literal hover, she still didn't want to be naked with the lights on and I respected this. The lights were out before the underwear came off.

The room would not be pitch black, moonlight could creep in, there was a streetlight on the next lot, once in a while she'd allow a small candle to flicker. It forced me into a tactile dimension where I had to imagine her ass by its contour and her snatch by its scent. I knew her nipples were large and dark, dense. Breasts low-slung with a pleasing uptilt. Her hips were fleshed over and smooth but still perceptibly forming a basin for her compact pussy. It seemed her clit was snuggled up to her pussy, barely covered by her shallow mound. It was easy to involve that nub in our lovemaking.

She did let me nudge her butt cheeks open when she was on downers, once in a while she'd relax enough to let me prod at the hole there incidentally/accidentally for a few minutes but she was adamant there'd be no actual butt sex. She indulged my request for this type of arousal because I was so cooperative about the lack of visual nudity.

At her request, I wore a leather blindfold one night so she could see me in the mirror naked and fucking her. I helped her set up. I felt foolishly excited by this concept: used by her, serving her. Once readied, I couldn't see a thing, no sliver of movement, no shadow shapes. I especially liked when she got astride me and I felt her swivel so I knew she was looking back over her shoulder at the mirror to watch her backside plunging on me and off me. I could imagine what it looked like from what it felt like for me to be her platform.

I reached up and pressed her breasts back against her ribs, holding her there, she had solid-feeling flesh that filled my palms. She'd lift herself into my hands, shoving her belly down tight against me and arching her back so I had the sensation of capturing her in flight. I'd thumb her nipples until I felt it in her pussy.

⌂ ⇩ ⌂

I remember losing a job because the owner of the store had decided that I thought he was stupid. I hadn't thought he was stupid until he promoted a lesser-skilled individual to a job I had applied for. That was stupid. I didn't react immediately, I was the same old me at the store; however, on my own time I was experiencing new emotions. I had not previously exhibited any particular ambitions other than to be employed gainfully and to not wear a suit. My application for promotion from assistant manager to manager should have been approved on merit and it surprised me when that wasn't the criterion. After thinking it over, I wanted to make a lateral move out of the store, into a different chain of retailers, just when the chance to work an owner/operator hardware store came up. The job was for exactly one year. The guy wanted somebody to run his store just the way it was always run while he was in federal prison for fifty-one weeks. I was to restock exactly as it was laid out and to turn all receipts over to his new accountant.

He told me, "I don't need somebody with ideas about hardware. I got what people need in here. I need somebody who's worked in a store—and you have. When I get back, though… I won't be needing you." He looked me over, to see if I'd flinch.

I told him, "I wouldn't mind a break from the food business, still, I do need a job. This should work out for both of us. The truth is, I've got an ulterior motive. If I'm going to distinguish myself in retailing, I need fresh ideas. Your store has always been interesting to me, it's a lot of simplicity."

"That's right. Nothing in here but hardware -- handy gadgets and supplies."

"You explained the IRS problem was related to your investments and not to the store. I want to make it clear I'm not tolerating any risk to my reputation, I'm really going to work the merchandise and not the money."

"Like you said, you've shopped here for years. What you see is what you get, nuts and bolts and hoses and clamps. Bulbs, tubes. It moves fast, you'll be busy. Spanners, sanders. My secret is that big parking lot, I get rent from the coffee hut and key shop plus a cut of the Christmas tree sales and pumpkin patch, it's customer friendly. The store's been hopping ever since I bought that lot. That turned out to be my problem, too much profit. What did I know about construction accounting? I'm a vendor, not a lender. Learned my lesson. Prison is nothing compared to people thinking I'm a crook. I got nabbed for unreported income taxes that I would have paid back when I had the money if I'd been smart enough to understand I owed them."

"Personally, sir, I pretty much stick to pay-check accounting. At the store, I can balance the cash, I can report the payables and receivables. The rest stays out of my hands."

"We're in agreement then, I can give you twenty-one days notice to start, it will be within the month. That's the notice I get when a spot opens for me. Fifty-one weeks is with good behavior and I'm going to behave. You better too!"

"I'm punctual, reliable, industrious and in the mood for this move. I'm sorry for your troubles."

"Lesson learned, my young friend, and one you might do well to learn by osmosis. It's a bitch head-on."

I find hash annoying. It's a sticky ball of happiness, sure. But you have to scrape each of your hits off, and if it's dry then you risk your fingers prying apart a resin-rock with the knife. I tried scraping pieces in advance but they seemed to diminish in size and potency after an hour or two. You need a screen on the pipe. You need to empty the screen of the unburnable impurities. You need a good pipe lighter since you'll be refiring it repeatedly. In the by-gone days it was something to do at a party, being the hash guy, preparing a bowl for a friend or a stranger, showing off by pre-warming the chunk just enough to make it easy to slice off a hit. As a loner stoner, I find it tedious.

I forget how tedious getting the hash pipe ready can be when I find myself longing for the creamy high of a stout bowl, best with a fresh screen, the peculiar taste of hashish that can't be faked. It can be perfumed and polluted but the underlying smoke is different than any other. Many manifestations of the high given the range in quality but, always, a hash high. Perfect for the solitary toker.

Hash gives a head high, you can feel it beneath your face, behind your forehead and, oddly, at the back of your teeth. It pulls sensation deep into the skull which then refracts out the eyes and slides off the tongue. I like it.

                    ↱ ⇩ ↘

    I discovered the hardware store's neighbor was a caterer when she came to pay her rent on part of the parking lot (she only needed the two spaces in front of her door at the far corner of the building). She'd hire staff to serve at functions held away from the premises, but she did the cooking and arranging herself. I was the beneficiary of her culinary experiments… I finally learned to savor bleu cheese and appreciate cooking wine. In a neighborly way, I treated her to various items of hardware from the store (I bought it at my employee discount). I'd watch her work, whisking and kneading, chopping, tearing… the food came alive for her.

    We were thrown together by the coincidental location of our business concerns. She did all the work and got half the profit, her brother covered the rent and utilities for his half and opened a line of credit for supplies. She seemed pleased with the arrangement because the place was an expression of her whole life. It was built from daily toil, it could be measured (in cups, in spoons), it was of her.

    Ming suspected she was lesbian but felt no impetus to test. Her life at home had been virginal, as it was expected to be. Her brother took over her care at the death of their parents. She owned a two-bedroom condo not far from the shop, her parents' legacy as directed in their wills. She was to select a proper home with acceptable amenities (security, parking garage, on-site management) and buy it outright then establish a fund for the foreseeable maintenance and taxes (plus contingencies). She could buy it if her brother approved specifically of its suitable nature. How careful her parents were!

    I seemed wild and free to her, partly because I was a man and an American man at that. She and her brother had been born in Hong Kong but got here young enough to have local vocabulary to express her quaint view of familial love. She was slim, black haired, almond-eyed… it made me feel very Occidental. Inviting rejection, I held her close to me one night. She stiffened and I backed away, that answered the unvoiced question. She introduced the topic of desire when she'd become aware of my rich and varied love life. I munched on left-overs while she balanced her daily books then we'd take a long stroll to unwind together. We did this only twice a week, the nights she never accepted late bookings (Tuesday and Thursday).

Perhaps because we were shoulder to shoulder, not eye to eye, we walked and talked easily; maybe it was the calming night breezes— something caused us to reach a conversational intimacy not possible when we were at her work place. When I asked about her love life, her laugh was cheerless.

"I never did like a boy that way."

"Nor a man?"

"You're all boys. Big bad boys. My solemn father? Prankster. Respectable brother loves the Three Stooges. Chinese men take advantage of their wives' kindness. You all disrespect women yet want them to love you."

"You sound pretty experienced to me."

"I can read. I can see. I really don't understand the drive that pushes women toward men."

"Women driven toward women, then? Do you feel that way, Ming?"

"I used to wonder, now I don't even do that."

"Hugs? Touch? Warmth?"

"I feel good walking with you."

"There's so much more."

"I have what I want."

"Then, be happy."

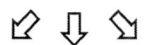

I fantasized about Ming. I fantasized about Princess Caroline of Monaco. I didn't mean to invade their privacy, I didn't always see their faces, at first (or at all). They were an embodiment of all that I longed for in my life: sizzle, balm, base, catalyst. I wanted to sink between gargantuan breasts that fit in the palm of my hand. Hurling towards peace.

So many aspects to the fantasies, the physical details, the sensuous cues, ohh, how I moaned at the thought of lickety-licking Miss November and/or June.

These women wanted me, they came to my side, they inhabited my head. Laverne with the lights low, monogrammed sweater lifted. Mrs. Robinson when she was young. Jamie Lee Curtis in her snippy mode. We kissed and danced and stretched out in front of fires, there was snow and surf and noon moonlight (it's a feeling). How fresh the women smelled. How firm the surface, how soft inside. How many ways have I been able to imagine giving them what they wanted, taking what they offered, making a world behind my closed eyes?

Ming, in my fantasies, insisted on only hints of sex, I'd think of her swimming, I'd think of her bathing, these were flashes of her in longer fantasies about other women. It was the way my mind worked, it slipped gears as I got more excited, a new face, a different mood, some other element, my treasured kaleidoscope.

There were nights I had to accelerate the images because I wanted to boil, I had to get agitated, the women would tease me, resist what they asked for, push me and prod me. I didn't pay attention to the action of my hands, I gathered energy in my throat, groaning and grunting, then swallowed it. It turned into heat, and blood zinged around my corners. My mind saw my hand tangled in long hair, pulling a dark-throated beauty up tight against my chest, her ear filled with my spoken commands.

"Sweet baby, honey bitch, be daddy's little devil… you like to growl, you like to signal. I can smell you; you're my fuckin' beacon. I've been lost in the cold, lonely dark then I sense you shining. Turn it on, lover, bring me home to you. Save me from myself! Call to me, sing out, sweetheart. Who has the hottest ass? Who sticks out her fanny for me to admire? Your spread legs are a dare.

"I love this, the start… my every urge is to plunge but I won't. Your cunt is tight, shy, mine! We're past playtime and I want your fullest and deepest sensation. I can inch myself all the way into you, just this slow and just this steady. Feel yourself give way? That's my pretty pussy, isn't it? Fit to fuck. Deep, wild, alien. You are what I miss, I am truly alive with you .

"Open yourself to me, embrace me, lover, bury me in your body."

Ming met a woman at a Japanese grocery. Ming told me, later, that the contact between them was electric. They talked in the parking lot for forty-five minutes before going out to dinner. Julie was French, adrift in her life. They were a world unto themselves. Julie was bi-curious and brought much of the heterosexual world into bed with them. Ming confided that Julie liked to fuck her, and especially liked to make her come that way. It was almost like a trick on all the men who longed for such a treasure and here, now, Julie possessed it with a flick of her wrist and a twitch of her lip…

For Ming, this was more than she'd ever dreamed of experiencing. It was so intense she was moved to speak to me of it, fearing it was unnatural to feel such pangs of desire, she'd lose time remembering Julie's lips on her nipples, the first such suckling ever! Ever! And the pinches!! Twisting!!! How cruel that nature indulged in extremes… passion was cresting in her.

"Ming, everybody is suspicious of their sex feelings. It doesn't matter why Julie makes you feel hot. She sees it in you, she brings it out. There is nothing for you to worry about. You're telescoping many major events into a single affair. Your first deep kisses, your first petting, your first fingering."

"I had nothing to confess before this. I may never have this again, it is the richest reward for following my fate. Julie is one kind of luck. Your friendship is another kind of luck."

"It's your time to flower, Ming. It's exciting to watch. I thought I'd be jealous if you found somebody to love but I'm thrilled for you. It makes you even more beautiful."

"Here's something weird. Julie wants to play doctor and test the temperature in my vagina."

"Wow, that's an interesting image."

"I think so too. Where do I get a hospital gown before Tuesday?"

I got a season's free weed by being part of a leaf cleaning crew when some guy's plants came in. We were picked up in a closed van, driven around until we ended up in a warehouse where we removed wax paper from the shorn plants, and were shown how to part the buds from the stalks. We wore latex gloves and had to change them every other hour because the resin collected on them. We worked for seven hours, and two weeks later we got paid in dried product. It was sweet bud with a clean smell and it consistently hit the mark. I knew going into the situation that it was a one-time deal. Six strangers steeped in nature's bounty.

It was hypnotic to handle that much marijuana. It was like counting somebody else's money. The plants were healthy, innocent, nipped in the bud… harvested. I was handling a commodity. It was just material. I could have been soldering circuit boards but, no, this was the rich reward of a season's growing.

We weren't encouraged to share our personal stories in the van and, once working, there was no time for chatting. We wore white coveralls without pockets, surgical booties, and skullcaps. They had set up three air filtering machines running on gas generators and still the air was thick. We'd never pass even a cursory inspection but somehow I knew these people had arranged a good spot for some fast processing. I didn't know why some of the plants looked hacked down rather than reaped (as if I'd know the difference). In the middle of the shift I didn't think I could go on. We were fed salads, bread and fruits then a quick walk around the building that provided an excellent second wind. The last half of the shift was definitely trippier. It looked like we were going to make it, and get this stuff preened and back on the road. [I wondered where the leavings were going.]

As a surprise, a generous-yet-discreet bag of shake was given to each of us before we got out of the van at the drop off point near a cab stand downtown (no driving home). These loose leaves had collected under and around the tables while we worked, each table stood in the center of a large wading pool that they periodically swept (new whisk brooms and dust pans, of course). I hadn't figured on anything so generous and upped my estimate of the crop's value. I couldn't have stood the stress of dealing for a living, although I was glad to participate in this preening. It wasn't romantic, it was like stocking shelves, stuff you had to do to get what you wanted.

↗ ⬇ ↘

For a while, I had the best store assistant in the world. Maureen played the piano for ragtime bands, it was like a religion with her. If she wasn't at the store she was entertaining somewhere. Schools, zoos, retirement villages, mall openings… her off-hours were spent in this musical sub-world. At work, she was spooky psychic with me. Things I hoped for happened, random ideas of mine were somehow silently communicated to her. I knew as a manager that I had to provide consistent expectations if I was ever going to get the cooperation of a team. Simple, unstoppable. We buy at a good price and sell at a fair price. We add value with service, the fruit is clean, we don't over-water the vegetables, the aisles are tidy, the signage is clear. I let Maureen talk straight with me. When the cashiers were ganging up on the courtesy clerks, I took her advice and gave the clerks a "keep a secret" weekly bonus. As long as no word leaked out of their secret, the bonus continued. It gave them, as a group, a collusive bond. It set them apart and held them together. Their air of shared mystery frosted the cashiers then Maureen stepped in and broke up the clique. It takes only a few people to turn a crew. In this case, like many, there was the obvious ringleader but, as usual, behind her worked the mind of another. Maureen saw it long before I did and eased us out of the situation by promoting the ringleader to an office job. As we expected Ms. Mock-iavelli, as we called her privately, didn't like working alone in the office and flounced out to try her hand at selling real estate.

↗ ⇩ ↘

Maureen was plain as plain could be. Limp brown hair, small brown eyes, beak nose, straight lips, medium build, no chest to speak of, flat assed, thick legged. Clothes never fit, she was always on the verge of squirming against the fabric. In me she saw a good guy, she told me that more than once. She'd been date raped and impregnated at college. Afraid to tell her parents, horrified and alone, she'd gone to a crisis center. She miscarried at four weeks, as if her womb ignored the implanted fetus and filled then flushed on its regular cycle. She felt a subtle pop inside, a peculiar sensation never felt before or since, and she let go of the idea of a baby. Instead, she got help with her feelings about the crime against her, and earlier fears about men and sex. She couldn't believe he'd gotten her pregnant since most of his "manhood" slimed down her leg. He had seemed nice as pie on their first date but the second ended against the hood of his car after a picnic. He had maneuvered her against the car, fumbling at her breasts, and she was afraid of being rude (!) since they were alone so far from town. He had bad breath and a small, bent dick. Afterwards, he shut down, didn't talk to her, drove her home and said, "I don't know what came over me." She didn't bother to correct him: he came all over her. Maureen concentrated on getting out of the car and into her dorm before disintegrating. She eventually called the resident advisor who wasn't much help, insisting Maureen didn't look traumatized, no bruises, no scratches. I imagine she looked like a statue, marble-hard with shame and rage and the guilty exultation of a survivor. Her bravest moment was seeking help, a second time, at the clinic. Something was wrong, she had to right it.

Maureen told me this because she asked that I walk her to her car each evening, and we instituted a buddy system for all employees. This revelation showed her trust in me, because all these years later something curdled in her when she was alone with a man. I knew she trusted me like a brother, she always teased me about various customers who made a point to say hello to me… could I demonstrate how to thump these melons? Was the meat prime? On the other hand, Margaret and I weren't the office romance types so she could expect me to serve my long-term career goals and thus stay true to the friendship.

Her story – once she spoke it out – was familiar, that is partly why I hated it. Men can be monstrous and it ruins the necessary balance between the genders. I liked to think of ravishing a woman (like Sundance did the teacher in *Butch Cassidy*) (oh, the power of pretend) but I don't think of violence, duress applied for sex is no different than similar crimes: robbery or assault, felonies. Rape is lower-order behavior, it is wrong, it is self-defeating. The true contempt to show a weak woman is to refuse to do her— she won't reproduce and her genes would wash away (existential nullification). If you tell men they are raping the strong women because of fear they get mad and rape again. The majority of men aren't rapists, but by a vast majority rapists are men. It chills when contemplated.

I've wrestled sexually with women but it was not a first-time, uninvited scenario. It would be a case of "oh, dear, you beastly brute, you nasty man, you ravaging cad" rather than "no, never ever, NO, get off me right now." We'd be rolling on the living room floor, pinning each other to the carpet, cooperating in a tussle. That can be fun, it loosens inhibitions. It can evolve into sexuous contact *by consent*.

I've heard shy confessions of a feminine desire to be… taken. It is the romance novel seduction of a competent female by the brawny, silent, mysterious male. Her dismay at the inexplicable power of his presence forces her to face her wild tides! It is hard for me to imagine being a woman in this man's world, where male cops pick up male perpetrators to face male juries in front of male judges. Women may have made some progress in the front lines but at heart we've got our white daddies in D.C., leading us to independence, pioneering, integration… revolution, civil war, world war, nuclear war, cold war, eco-war. Men like me can admit some of our brothers are dogs, and some are pigs…but most of us are just men.

I'm the guy who helps his mother with her spring cleaning projects, I'm the guy who attends his nephews' sports and recitals, I'm the guy who likes to sit in the window of a coffee shop with a lovely lady and laugh. I'm not shy with women I know, I'm the guy they can talk to about anything. I'm a guy at ease.

It isn't impossible for me to imagine some of the forces involved in violence between men and women, the "got to do this" part of the human brain blocks out counterthoughts. Violence is selfish, it denies the presence of another complete being. The target/victim/thing isn't on the same plane as the all-consuming me-need – the target is or has the thing wanted. When people refer to true crime books, I'm with those who think true detective. We want our protectors to win. We're uneasy when things aren't solved. Who did what? If we know who, we (think we) know who didn't so we (think we) can breathe easier.

Maureen believes she's taken a big step by being friends with me, we're linked and know some truth about each other. She'd never want to sleep with me, she said, but she understood how other women would. Insight like that helps wear down the rough edges left by her hurtful initiation into human sex, she can admit intellectually that not all men are scum and even joke that it's too bad 99% ruin it for the rest of them.

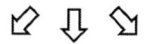

"Where were you when Lennon died?"
"Lenin? I wasn't even born yet. How old do you think I am?"

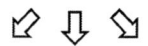

Perhaps I'd be a howling wolf without my habitual marijuana use. In research of the weed, I had to group myself statistically with chronic users. I knew the ganga-laden Rastafarians were leagues beyond me (hail, Ras Tafari, Lion of Judah); I knew I was far left of the citizens' center on this personal freedom. Pot laws got me revved up on ideas of religion, philosophy, freedom of expression, pursuit of happiness, inalienably mine as a human citizen. And tax revenue. I might be too short to play professional basketball and too far from Hollywood for the movie industry yet still marry a President's widow. I might have gulped gallons of jug wine, tooted a cloud's worth of coke, chipped in shots of speed or worse. Nah! Didn't click with my chemistry. If you ask me, I'll tell you I'm having a good life with no major complaints.

Why I'm not twisted up like so many others seem to be is beyond me. I have a regular family and wasn't molested by my coach, school seemed OK to me, I was heavy into nature as a boy and considered bullies were like cheetahs and the innocent were gazelles, learned life is tough. I was some sturdy sort of animal who didn't attract much notice in the jungle of life, maybe a dam-building beaver, industrious and prudent -- more of a woods and water dweller than the extreme personalities of the wild. How could I not feel like a lucky guy? I had a home, I had friends, I fell in and out of love and lust without severe consequences. I'm sure there are millions of you who feel the same: a sigh of relief that overall you'd landed on a lucky number.

I'm an Aquarian, smack dab in the center of a creative, intuitive sign and yet I'm solid as a rock, very American. I'm not unwilling to explore the idea of celestial destiny. If I'd been born in 1400, my stars would have aligned much differently. I did get the distinct impression my current incarnation was suited to survive and thrive. The Viet baby born in a rice paddy at the same instant had different stars. Longitude + Latitude. I was delivered to a (predominantly) free land still working on its essential constitution. My grandparents were run out of their home country and landed in Iowa, sponsored by a church, working a rented farm until they owned it. They were distant cousins but nobody in America knew that, they were presumed to be married because they arrived on the same scummy ship with the same last name; thus my dad always joked he is an inbred bastard since as immigrants his parents were afraid to bring

Kathleen K.

attention to themselves by explaining the misperception by Immigration officials. What if speaking up as being single cousins cancelled their applications due to closer scrutiny? Afterwards, settled here, how could they court and marry other people after they had been presumed to be spouses? It was a fertile partnership. This land, this America, gave them a home and sheltered their children. My Aunt Nicole found out their genealogy and by the time I was old enough to understand the implications, they were dead and it was nobody's business outside the family. Still, I was raised to praise the U.S.A. because individuals could survive on wits and work.

I was infuriated by racism because it was viscerally wrong, it doesn't make sense. Saw the pattern repeat with hispanics, with asians, once they gathered in sufficient numbers to be noticed. My country has ducked its head on this struggle, falling victim to the violent believers of a dead idea: white men alone hold the human torch. Fools. They're dangerous like bacteria replicating mindlessly, puny dirt threatening larger life. We fail to unify and thus weaken ourselves. Governments do it, individuals do it.

In my own way, I'm fighting to be true. It's been a while since I expressed myself about the godness around us, evident in the beetle, the cloud, the poppy. This may be a biochemical string of events, fine... science can explain what happened once the primordial stuff was here but so far no word on the transitional moment before there *was* that stuff... our science is of action and reaction. What started it is debatable. There's a known limit to spontaneous combustion, meaning you have to have some combustibles first.

What each little life means, I don't know. It's pretty obvious you should grab some gusto, there is thrill in living. Run fast, eat good, sleep tight. There is a moral line, the exact position of which may be in dispute, conceded in the main as don't kill and, otherwise, mind your own business. Given the enchanting existence of our "personality", how can we waste it hating others who find themselves as mysteriously made flesh (of whatever shade)? In a way, it is because we are so overendowed with survival skills that we topple in the other direction, making wars and abusing our families. We so fervently want to survive that we imagine threats to keep sharp. What a conundrum it is to the human race who tames the elements by fission science that peace retards progress while war retards life… but what is life without progress? Is it really progress or aimless movement? Or is it just life? Finite in specific, infinite in scope.

What will humanity achieve once it stops the cave-raids on its neighbors? Cultivate food, let the earth take care of itself (quit paving it!) and exploit our post-simian cleverness. What could we do if we simply fed our poor? Nothing more than laying out food for anybody who wants to eat. No forms to fill out. Who can bridge the continental gaps so we work as a globe on this? Food. And a bed. Still too soon for that, it seems, although it looks like technology may be its voice. I've used computers at the store enough to know they are good little robots, dutifully carrying the user forward faster. Inventory is a good purpose for a computer and I appreciated the usefulness of mine. I could see its organizational potential which made me think of hives, buzzing with ritual life. I read enough science fiction to accept the idea of networking. I am not a prophet: I did not foresee teen sex chat rooms.

↗ ⇩ ↘

SssssssssssssssssssssssssssssssssssssssssssssssssssssssssssssssssssssssssssssssssssssssssssssssssssssSssssss…

The opposite of fricative, a hot hiss, air streaming over the fluted tongue past the parted lips, the sound of LaLinda when we made love. I remember that sound when I think of my beautiful friend. I couldn't hold her to me forever, I couldn't have withstood the regrets at the end of her life when she inevitably realizes she can't experience all that she desires. I would've been blamed for blocking her way (anyone would). I am guilty of not taking those parts of her that were actually made for me but it would have crippled us both to join even for a while. Maybe it's my Aquarian side showing, I saw the art in her freedom.

Her nipples shriveled when I licked them. I'd listen for her sigh and get my hand against her mound so she could know the hunger was in me too. Her trust made me feel good, it wasn't always love between us, sometimes comfort, sometimes convenience, sometimes erotic pique. Still, I waited for her to sizzle up. In a particularly good mood, she might mash her breasts together for me, so the nipples could be gotten in one lick. That seemed to stimulate us both, reverberating. In my own way, I longed for a more complete bonding mentally but on the physical plane did not doubt our integral connexion. She would shudder in my arms from being fingered, lightly. She often cried out which shook my dick, I can tell you. These weren't those fake breathy *oooh*, *ooohs* we pretend signify sex, LaLinda grunted and groaned, cursed, cried, laughed, exploded. I'd feel the powerful heaving muscle between her legs, contorting with life. She'd cling to me for a minute or more then draw back to drain away the final paroxysms. She'd hug herself and I'd be so damn glad to be alive.

Then it would be my turn.

LaLinda would kneel at the edge of the bed, her backside poised in space, so I could brace my legs against the mattress and pull her against my cock. She was weightless in this position, of substance but no pressure. I'd hold her hips and watch my cock pop in and out of her. She'd dip her chest down against the bed so her ass flared at me, her back smoothly rounded to her shoulders. If she lifted her shoulders, I'd reach around and feel her boobs dangling, she hummed which I found ridiculously sexy when I was shoved to the hilt in her pussy. She seems to lengthen inside, as if she's smoothed the passage closer to her core, when she was spread just right I swear I could feel the head of my prick drumming between her ribs. I couldn't get enough of that feeling, engorged inside.

LaLinda liked to be able to look over to her mirrored headboard when I went down on her, she played with her breasts with one hand and put her other hand on my head to keep me firmly in her crotch. It was my habit to spread her lips with my thumbs but at the beginning I started by licking the closed seam of her cunt and mouthed her pussy lips. She was shy about this every time, she was paranoid about "being fresh". It was my duty to inform her beforehand if it was my intention to eat her and then her preparations took a few minutes longer. I wasn't fool enough to ask why it was OK to finger and fuck her lesser-prepared pussy; I knew she had a horror of sex during her period, she felt (and then acted) unclean. Conversations about menstrual sex were cut short. Some do, some don't, she didn't.

It was only after I'd gotten my tongue deep in her hole that she would admit that she was glad to be spread and devoured, she described fantasies of being eaten to a dead faint, eyes drifting back in her head, tongue lolling. She claimed she dreamed of being eaten at the opera. It was her idea to put a wooden foot stool at the side of the bed so I could sit with her legs up over my shoulders and "drive" her with the upturned palms of my hands upon which danced her flexing behind.

She showed such honest emotion that I couldn't bear to do less. I was a hound for her cunt and enjoyed every moment she granted me.

I know some guys act as if cunnilingus was not an option for "real men" (who, as we've been told, don't eat quiche either). Cannot agree. I am sure there are those that don't, or aren't granted the pleasure, but it is my distinct impression from the women I know that many men find fulfillment face-forward between feminine thighs. If there is any more central distinction between the genders than genitals, it could only be the brain. Since we don't understand the brain completely, I'll withhold judgment on that. I have seen much evidence regarding the genital area of males and females, including some info on the blended genders of hermaphrodites, and I stand firm— different form, different function, common goals. Males spread seed, females collect seed, with the common goal of furthering the race. Once past that reproductive imperative, men outproduce women's egg production by about a kabillion to five hundred (thirteen eggs a year times forty years, averaged out for non-menstruation due to pregnancy, illness, etc.). The biological clock is more a matter of emptying egg cartons, starting with them stacked in the "warehouse" then egg by egg, carton by crate by shelf they escape and tumble down to the uterus to meet any passing sperm or else be flushed to the sea.

Whether met or not, that egg has had its chance. When the eggs are gone, the delivery machine shuts down, by the mid-fifties, unless a fertilized egg is borrowed and implanted, that woman is free of reproductive risk, loses her ability to create life. Period. (Or, more accurately, no period)

Men can produce seeds on their deathbed, not as often, perhaps not as much, but, if left uninjured, there is a chance to be an eighty-year old sperminator. Women do not work like that. That is a big difference, although how it ties in to women living longer and men going to war isn't completely understood. Rushing about in response to hormones isn't much different than being victims of the "humours" and "vapors" that were credited with affecting human behavior... we want to talk about WILL, about CHARACTER, about our SELFHOOD. We may be walking talking chemical factories churning up a bunch of electrolytes and blood gases, but we stress our FEELINGS and our THOUGHTS. We're mapping the brain but getting no closer to the lightning-like process of ideas being born.

I'm fascinated by studies on comparative biology, especially accounts of differences in the male and female brain, but we're so obviously parts of a whole that it is a waste of time to differentiate whether one is more or less human. For that is the crux of it, are men "more" human, are their traits inherently superior, is it to be measured by the impact on survival (when we need far fewer males to service breeding females then do women rank higher)? I like the idea that a person's worth transcends gender even as I realize that their accomplishments may be proscribed by gender relative to time (how many political women have been denied by custom in their era the chance to compete for public office?). In how many societies have they been or are they now extensions of a property system?

This kind of thinking lets me have great discussions with women, because I consider this topic of value. My manhood is a part of me but it shows most clearly against the foil of womanly presence. I challenge myself to set aside the presumptions of my male-habituated thoughts and *listen*. I hear you, ladies. You're richer and sweeter and more bitter than men admit. You cannot trust men to respect your agenda let alone advance it. You are seasonal and cyclical and variable. There are boys, men, and old boys.

↗ ⬇ ↘

I had a dual hookah for a while, but it was broken by a person who shall be nameless, who promised to replace it. And I'm still waiting.

↗ ⬇ ↘

"Lick it up, lick it up, come on, lick it like you like it, lick it like you care. Suck it up, eat it up, eat my raging cock like I eat your weeping pussy, let me fill your pretty face. Take it in until I feel your chin, fill your throat with the taste of me. Yeah, love, go, love, love me with your lips, love me with your tongue. Love me like I love you, all the way."

Sex talk turns me on. I like to hear it, I like to say it, I like to read it (I'm learning to write it). I got my first real lesson in this from a certain woman who would eat me as long as I talked and she would stop when I stopped talking. I finally figured out the pattern— Pavlov would be proud— and was astounded at all the words dammed behind my teeth, which I previously clenched while being fellated. I worked at keeping my verbal center going when all other energies were pooled beneath my belly. It wasn't easy, sometimes I could only grunt meaningfully and if she was in the mood then she considered that feedback enough. It was somewhat like masturbating in the sense I had to supply the connections in the imagery.

I usually pulled out and ejaculated on her throat and breasts, she was more agreeable to providing sublime oral stimulation if I withdrew for the finale. This external culmination was like so many porn movies that it felt natural, she always smiled real pretty when I came, and since there is nothing quite like getting face I was hardly going to skip the many minutes of excitation to claim an internal target for one specific spurt at the end.

Kathleen K.

As she well knew, the times she held me in and I poured down inside her throat were even more precious for their rarity. Prized moments when I felt ferocious, I felt consumed.

Perhaps not all men feel this way. Some are shortsighted and, by not reaching for new experiences, catch far fewer opportunities.

Yes, there are bad blow jobs. I've had a few. But then again... too few to mention.

I don't like shoplifters. Naturally, as a store manager, I do prefer theft be small scale and low key. The risk of armed robbery rises to the level of a life threat while shoplifters, individually, are a nuisance. It is my preference to have door security to discourage robberies and I budget an off-duty cop twenty-four hours a day. It is an investment in safety and courtesy, as I explained to the owners of the store. Nothing is more terrifying than a robber thrown in with customers and workers... even though all the people who work for me have simple instructions: (1) open till, (2) scoop out money, (3) avoid confrontation. I fear the unpredictability of a customer/would-be-hero's reactions. The money is nothing and not just because it is all insured. We use a special courier service for the cash (of which there is less and less these days) which does not pull up in an obviously armored vehicle. I deal with bonded delivery and pickup people and how they travel is their business, but I like their style. They're ingenious which is a good element in security.

I've not been hit by robbers but tons of stuff is lifted from the shelf and wanders out the door without being rung up at a register. People pack meat in their pants and apples under their hats, we catch people with drop pockets full of spices or fish food (popular because they are expensive by the ounce, these items are targeted by semi-pros who are 'shopping' for a cheating retailer or wholesaler).

Once in a while we get a senile senior who repeatedly appears, we get to know their family when they come to escort the offender home.

I'm not immune to letting a few cans of tuna fall into a pensioner's purse except a pang of concern that they risk so much for so little. Teenagers are ridiculous, inept and over-confident. In those cases, the security cop calls for a patrol car on low priority, then sits with the youthful offender(s) in silence. If they ask about the upcoming process, they are told no information is available from us *by law*... it becomes an *official* police matter and we will quietly sit and wait for those police to arrive. In fact, a juvenile department officer team is dispatched when possible. These young thieves have all seen too many movies and try to bluff and tough it out. They're going to sue for false arrest, their parents have important friends, they didn't do it, and if there is proof they did, they didn't mean it.

There's perplexing middle-aged offenders, they have plenty of money for what they need, even for what they want, but they steal. They're copping a thrill at my expense (but they're not thinking about me or anybody else, it's a selfish inward act). I can only imagine how sophisticated the pros are at jewelry stores and other rich targets. Big ticket merchandisers have it worse because, face it, it's rare any item in our grocery store is worth more than $50.

To help my marginal customers, I frequently run specials on items like eggs, diapers, flour and sugar, diarrhea medicine (I swear I think it is shyness, not greed, motivating the boosting of this particular item). I understand a strained budget. Essentials should be carried by the higher margin on choice items.

I did have a dishonest warehouseman for a while; I was slow to accept the obvious increase in loss after his arrival. Hickings was a nice guy, and he stayed on top of things. My inexperience led me to expect a thief to be shifty and bad at his work. Not so with Hickings. His method wasn't creative, it was based on bravado... he had his orders stapled to his delivery receipts, his logs were neatly written. Yet, here a case, there a case, every where a case gone. He never did confess, I confronted him and he narrowed his eyes then turned, got his coat and left. He never called for his final check (as if I was intending to pay him!). That was all the confession I needed at the moment, but I was glad the losses stopped after he was gone, confirming my instincts.

Kathleen K.

I am aware of the irony of my law-and-order stance at work while I break drug laws on my own time. What can I say? I did my job straight. And did my living in private.

"You gotta change the bong water, man."
"It's not just the water, the whole pipe's gunked up."
"You got any others?"
"… I actually do."
"So, … are you going to go get one?"
"I'll have to put water in it first."
"No, first you have to go get the pipe."
"Then I put the water in."
"That's right. Then give it to me because I don't think you need any more smoke."

I was thinking about my love life one spring day, it was my good fortune to have entwined myself with various females over the years. It perplexes me when men claim there are no good woman out there. What in the hell are they talking about? The world abounds with people, half of whom are female, some large percentage in any target age range exist for the seeking male (and there are men out here for you, ladies). It is true there are precious few that might qualify for a marriage/mating-for-life choice for any one particular man (or woman). That is probably a big part of the problem. Many people are so finely tuned to long term relationships they miss the opportunity for meaningful friendships that would never progress past the enriching experience they are. Fearful of missing their once in a lifetime person, they deny the many good moments due. And it is those moments that prepare you to appreciate a life-mate later.

I don't think I'm wrong to pursue the time of a woman just because I don't want to share pensions. I can take her swimming and we can eat hot dogs at a ball game and dance naked in the dark backyard. How many minutes in a life get devoted to the simple pleasure of somebody's company? In my experience, women who click with me are forthright about what they want. Some distinction lies in how they react if you don't qualify for the starring role of Groom, will they enjoy a few scenes with a supporting player? Can I be a naughty secret, the man who licked her spine? Will she be flattered to know that years from that moment, I will remember her in that moment? In a good way.

No one will convince me that these attractions are inconsequential. I can remember women I danced with once, they are in my mind, part of my heart, each has added a layer of perception to my view of women. When my eyes close and I project the happenings of my past, it excites me for the future.

Which is not to say I like all the women all of the time. I'm aware that covens of modern day witches survive, even thrive, on the lifeblood of the male. They bed him, wed him then want support for the rest of their lives. It is one thing for a wife of twenty years to demand her share of the community pot, it is another to see a three-year relationship equate to a long sentence of alimony. Times have shifted but not all the way, not even half the way.

All men aren't likable either, let me hasten to add. It makes me cringe to realize how many dads dump their kids, how many sons abandon their parents, how many husbands mistreat their wives. Worse, how many are not able to support themselves in life. They believe that the world owes them a living for being alive, they think people who work are jerks but they covet the things earned.

It is no wonder there is confusion between the sexes when each half is choked by years of inequity. Men worked so hard to keep women down, they didn't see themselves slipping into the mire. Now the planet is dirty, the fish are sick, we're blowing through fossil fuels like there is no tomorrow. Partly, that view is true. In many people's world view, their immediate existence is the measure of time. What will help me? How soon and for how long? History is boring and the future isn't going to help me now (*but see* Star Trek IV: The Voyage Home).

Sometimes I wonder what I would have done if I had a kid when I was nineteen, or twenty-nine. How would I have faced myself, the mother, my parents, the child? I was awed by people's audacity in siring children. How could they take on the utterly impossible task of preparing another person for life? Sure, the answer is that many do not view procreating in that light. They are wrong. To reproduce is the greatest conceit: there must be more of <u>me</u>. Perhaps I got hit with a killer dose of Zero Population Growth propaganda, it clicked in my head that making more humans was not on my agenda. The current cadre of humanity had enough to do trying to slow down then reverse a population explosion. There are a finite number of square miles on this orb of ours, and that number divided by the projected population is ridiculously small, too small a share to support an individual. [This flies in the face of pension systems which require a viable number of next generation contributors to support current beneficiaries.]

My family thinks I'm radical about this but maybe I'm just too lazy to haul my kid's snotty butt to soccer practice; I simply prefer not to have to face the bittersweet fact my innocent infant is going to be a grown up person like everybody else, scammin' and jammin' to find peace.

So kill me, I'd rather party.

I found a recipe for pot brownies that uses a lot of nuts and raisins so you don't notice the pot so much. Plain brownies filled with leafy dope make the contrast too stark in the mouth… sweet chocolate and gritty pot. One nutty batch fueled a train ride across the country, I was booked for a fifty-hour marathon with no long stops along the way where I could walk off and toke. Other drugs were not really cool enough for the train, I wanted the fuzzed-head hey-man-cool feeling of marijuana.

I was absolutely ripped during much of the ride, drinking coffee in the club room between meals, watching the globe go by out the window. The trip was a last hurrah after college. No car (no payments), no apartment (no rent), so I plunked half my last student-job paycheck on a train pass for the summer. I'd gotten old enough to not hitchhike when I wasn't in the mood. It was nice to be dry and warm in a leather-ette seat while the rain poured down on the people on the plains...

That long ride was landmark for me. I met people taking short hops (a couple hours). All us long riders were put in the farthest cars, the short timers were hustled in and out the middle. I'd drift through the cars and mingle when I felt like seeing if there was somebody to talk to for a while. It was obvious I wasn't going to bond with the retirees riding the rails, playing bridge and hearts, moving like a visitation of ordinariness. The couples were earnest, and the widows and widowers were even more exposed. One old woman told me she was shuttled endlessly between her four children, each in a different corner of the country, and the train rides were her only peace. Tolerated in return for her babysitting, she never felt honored, did not experience welcome for the fact she was the mother of these parents but rather was treated as nanny to the grandkids... perhaps she'd done something wrong that all four siblings scattered, using her as a courier of news on her quarterly visits. Maybe it was the times. And why did she let/make them define her life? Had she not prepared for a life of her own? Still, the grandkids were getting older and needing less help, she could see how she could relinquish her role gracefully, cut each visit by a week... eventually two... She could see that her son was quick to let her go after he got her to do what he needed to have done, her daughters were making their own homes and didn't appreciate her way of doing things. They wanted her to keep doing things, yes, but to do them as she was told to do them by the people she'd done for all her married life.

I met people my age, some in similar circumstances, some so alien I could only stare in amazement. One girl my age had five kids... the first at seventeen, and they were taking yet another journey down state to see her third husband, who was in jail. He only had eight months left on his auto theft conviction which only happened because he had taken a job in a chop shop to support her! Odd to say, I think she was motivated by love. He'd adopted her other children and had made arrangements for her to receive government benefits in addition to private money he had delivered to her through his cronies. When he got out, they were going to rent an old farm house and fix it up. They spent every visit planning. They studied carpentry books and read about spotting dry rot. The kids didn't seem unhappy that I could tell, but what do I know about kids? He had a job waiting at a franchise lube place so they'd be financed in the future. The idea of coming home to her and the kids every night made any job tolerable, or so he said. It made sense to her.

The only hardship on the train was not having a shower available, but I didn't work up a sweat during the trip and I changed clothes each morning… still, there is a relaxation of standards when on the train, who *really* cared – if you didn't get too close? My destinations were cheap motels where'd I'd shower, walk, shower, eat then sleep stretched out. Visit who ever I was there to see.

Therese told me it was a little known fact that starlight was the secret ingredient to breast firmness. We were on a hotel balcony at the ocean shore. It charmed me that she unbuttoned her own blouse and bared herself to the stars.

This wasn't a quick flash (although those *are* appreciated). She leaned her head back, exposing her throat and lifting her ribs, positioning her breasts with a roll of her shoulders. Her nipples rose in the breeze, pebbled and dark, while I admired the lift of her tit from the side, its generous undercurve, and the apparent firmness.

"Starlight."
"What, Therese?"

"Starlight does something to breasts, it nourishes them, they suck up the twinkle."

"Does it work on cocks?"

"You'd have to ask a warlock."

Therese liked to sniff a hit of coke right before we had sex. I never minded because it was an organic act peculiar to our intimate circumstances. In her travel bag she kept a silver canister containing apparently powerful cocaine. The top doubled as a snifter (you could also shake it onto the web of your thumb like salt for tequila).

We engaged in serious foreplay during which we were both straight, she very much enjoyed teasing and pleasing. However, we were always lightly clothed and remained that way. When we decided it was time to do the do, we'd retire to our respective corners and imbibe. I'd slam a few tokes out of my portable bong while she powdered her nose. I'd get naked then she would strip tease. What fun to watch her display herself, proud and flushed with acceptance, slender through the hips with great legs, shapely and long. I've already extolled her starlit tits…

Thinking of Therese, I wonder where she is and how she is. It's been years and years since she moved away. I don't know how to say it… I don't "miss" her but she holds a place in my heart. I toss out good thoughts to her like pennies in a wishing well, just in case.

I've been "optioned" by the grocery company to set up a store in another city, I'm supposed to pick the manager and show him/her how to assemble a crew and operate a store. We'll use the schedules I invented and the forms I designed to track the facts of the business. I wrangled an extra week's vacation in the deal so I'm taking a car trip before I arrive there for three weeks, come back here for two weeks then back there for two weeks.

This is great! I needed a break from my store, a little shake-up. Everything hummed along and I got to feeling like a cog in a wheel – setting up a new place would give me a different position on the wheel if ever the cog I must be. It struck me that I'd been "faithful" to my store for a very long time, not moving beyond its circumstantial facts. In the new place, with the luxury of applying my experience, I'd be able to better understand what really made it work. Plus, I'd see how my system back home ran without me.

I'd taken a few business administration and accounting courses so there was a backbone of theory to my applied principles. It seemed to me that retailing groceries was cosmopolitan and socially useful. I wanted to look up over the edge of my rut and see if there was something more to do along those lines, while maintaining a firm grip on the division between making a living and having a life.

It was OK for me to aspire to more challenging work, I wasn't turning into a suit by any means. My work had to be rooted in the real world or I'd open up a horrible can of worms regarding the purpose of existence. As long as I could reach through my j.o.b. and stay connected to life and death, I was in balance.

On the other hand, it wasn't just the cash bonus or the week off that motivated me to try something new. I could envision being a regional manager, taking one step back from putting fresh baked biscuits in bags of six. I understood the bookkeeping, could sling a box blade, bagged scientifically; I was able to transfer this knowledge to others. I took pride in error-free payroll, my invoices are filed the day they arrive, every day is posted at the end of that day. I run the "day" from midnight to midnight then have graveyard accounting that takes four hours (this part-time job is easy to fill, lots of number-crunchers are night owls, three rotate with one sub; I can do it myself in a pinch).

I believe in dignity at work, I'm appalled when I read about the hostile environments encountered by so many: in the military, in government service, in the private sector. I'm spoiled by the ability to set the tone at the store. I encourage everybody to keep their mind on the store at the store, I don't like to clutter work relationships with too much personal info. The store is an oasis from your "real" life, you clock in and become part of the store until you leave clean and clear at the end of your shift. It is the best of routines because different things happen to change the moments but overall everybody has a purpose and time is kept faithfully..

Naturally you will find some people forming personal attachments ("special friendships") but in practice we all have to cooperate to get the food out the door and that comes first. What you do outside the store (well, not right outside the store's door…) has nothing to do with me if it doesn't manifest itself negatively at work. Else how would I know about it? I discourage personal phone calls except for the necessary check-in of kids after school, etc. Fifteen-minute breaks are required by law and twenty minutes off are necessary in practice, phones are provided in the break room… feel free to ignore the customers then and only then.

There is a respect for a worker's privacy, it shields us all. I've heard appalling conversations while waiting for service at the body shop or when checking in for a dental appointment. How can people blur their perspective, revealing themselves by bickering on the office phone as if everybody within earshot cared if Leroy took his own smelly cat to the vet. Why didn't their employers step in and advise them of more appropriate use of their time? A bit of the old stiff upper lip would also help. Tune out your clamoring life for a few hours and earn your living. Your problems (family/whatever) will still be there when you go back to that part of your life and at least you'll have earned some dough.

I pay store employees a bit extra because I get a bit more out of everybody than the usual employer. It is specifically pointed out as a condition of employment. If you were the sort who could do it, you were welcome to join us. If you weren't, you were welcome to go.

Once in a while I get a rooster, they land in the store and think they've done all that is required by showing up. The interview was the peak of their effort, not a preview. I was getting pretty good at spotting them but still they slipped in now and then, and squatted. Them wasting too much of my time didn't happen because I stopped it so early and firmly. It was

Kathleen K.

awkward in the sense we would have to discuss the hopelessness of them remaining. Since our agreement specifically (initialed) indicated the first ten days were strictly introductory and noncommittal, I never quibbled about whether it was fair. Most resisted the idea of having to look for another job "without warning". As specified (initialed), they were paid out on the spot. As explicitly agreed – signed and dated.

Sometimes I wanted to shake some sense into them about how they appeared to others (meaning me), they blithered and blathered about trying harder when we both knew they'd done what they thought was required and it wasn't enough. In my hiring, I'm careful to reserve an open channel for my opinion, that as manager I have the duty and the right to make choices. In some ways it wasn't always about the specific individual, but how they affected the crew as currently composed. It could be a lack of fit, an impossibility of circumstances.

The only times I've felt sick at heart were finding inside thieves, once a bookkeeper who deftly pocketed overages for two years, another a cashier who was under-ringing a small band of housewives who split the savings with her. Partly it was the petty nature of these transgressions, neither thief absconded with millions and retired to a private island, it was the disdain for simple fairness that depressed me. These were dirty acts, done with low cunning, repeatedly risked for proportionally little gain. It was the store owner's policy to file a police complaint on all such theft, although the company could elect to drop the charges later. I had an advisory role only, I didn't want anybody to think they could wheedle or deal out of the full experience. That was also specified (initialed) on their employment contracts at each annual renewal.

And, yes, ouch, I was taken for a fool, robbed by an associate, lied to, cheated. Of course I found that depressing. I paid top wages, finagled benefits from the ownership, investigated creative options like a discount at a nearby daycare in exchange for a discount on their supplies from our store. We also donated a Daycare Care Day when volunteers could go over and scrub and paint, wash toys, sort lost and found items for charity, update the donation list, whatever we could we did. In exchange, we also had an annual picnic with the kids and their parents which was *great* neighborhood bonding (and where did we buy the food – at cost?).

Why rip me off? But, of course, it wasn't about me. It was about them. They couldn't control their impulse to engage in subterfuge for pecuniary gain. Neither of these two examples was a hardship case, they weren't feeding eleven children living in a shoe, they just wanted a cushion without the mundane effort of earning it. They wanted something extra, because they were special.

They thought they were clever, yet were no smarter than crows hoarding gum wrappers, unable to articulate why they like shiny objects. In another way, it was substantial money in terms of being unaccounted for in taxes, or shared with a spouse, instant cash gave a boost to the budget, took the edge off. It isn't hard to imagine how nice it would be to have but we're taught that stealing for gain is wrong.

"It's kind of fun, not getting high."
"Changing things up is good."
"Sure it is, yeah. But your guy, he's coming later…?"
"Yep, then we can change back."

The store owners wanted to start an employees' college scholarship plan but I felt it was too restrictive. There were many lessons to be learned in life and not all occurred on a campus. Instead, I asked them to think up a "grant" program for matching funds. The applicant had to identify an educational/developmental goal, detail the steps to be taken to achieve it, and form a budget. The limit to match was $1,000 (later lifted to $2,000).

A cashier took paramedic training.

Kathleen K.

A bookkeeper took tax classes.

Another cashier trained in bicycle repair.

My warehouseman invested his grant in divinity school.

I applied for and was granted the funds for more business classes. It was practical on my part to cut the tuition through a grant, and I felt the deepening of my theoretical base would benefit the store. And perhaps propel me one rung up the ladder.

The "initiative grants" were a perfect vehicle to reward the motivated. No money was wasted on those who didn't try.

I went through one-hitter pipes every few months, doing minimal maintenance, until the active one got too sticky to use. I dropped it into some pipe cleaner and brought out another one, same shape and weight, fresh. I double-tap the bowl, sucking up the high, alone at home. I wander around, touching talismans, blowing dust off framed moments. This was my place, it held my things, it welcomed my visitors, and anchored me in the deepest way. I had freedom in this refuge, I was myself here.

Getting high before my walk meant I'd have to plan ahead, avoid distractions, stay true to the mind-altering I'd instigated, savor it. From my den to my door to the sidewalk then toward the residential section, away from the bakeries and bars and quickie marts and all those hellos. I was one of many people feeling at ease moving through a friendly neighborhood. I welcomed my thoughts against a backdrop of family life, toys on the lawn, grill on the back porch; all these other people were acting out the scenes I remember as a kid. I don't feel the need to pass this knowledge down to another generation, not like these others who are doing so every day. I'm glad 'community' exists and I can trust it to endure, it's our successful adaptation to tribal politics. I've got a clan, I pledge allegiance to the flag, I accept the modern way of life. I'm a frequent flyer in the head-osphere. I'm just as good at landing as I am at getting off.

"I am major mellowed out."
"It's a creeper weed. Sneaks up on you, it needs time to ripen."
"Ripe sounds good. I'm baked. Toasted. Completely completed."
"As long as you're not wasted."

I was surprised how many women expected me to start mooching once we were intimate. Evidently, lots of men slip this way. Since I believe each adult should have a way to sustain their own life, I was not in need of a "boost" from the budget of a lover. It would have offended me if I was expected to "assist" in the living expenses of some one else, whether or not it was for sexual access. That's part of the here-and-now for me. I can observe mooching as a fact but can't "feel" it for myself. It didn't bug me when I kicked in money for a new roof for my cousin's house because it was a tenth anniversary present. They could use their own hard-won roof savings for a surprise weekend honeymoon… that's how my family helps its people. Lift one burden. Wipe out one worry. Expect them to handle the rest.

I adopted a neighborhood nursing home and tithed to its general fund. It wasn't hard to explain to myself why I thought this was due… if those that could help did help, we'd eliminate some stresses on all of us. The donated ten percent seemed easy to calculate and was rooted in my idea of a worshipping society. I wasn't going to be attending any sermons soon but it didn't mean that I was exempt from good works. There are amenities not funded through Medicare that can make life easier for our seniors.

Would I be so generous if I didn't have the money? I am frugal by nature and legally unencumbered so it wasn't hard to relax into the comfort of sending in some off the top, like it was taxes, it made me feel like a citizen, not just a voter. If I earned less, I'd still tithe.

When I examine my character I know that this is a profound part of my value system, a basis for my other decisions. I don't know how other people feel but it is apparent that many of us compare ourself to what we think we ought to be and seek peace in our choices. At times I sit in my bedroom and feel so right-with-the-world that it's risky to acknowledge it (jinx it). My extended family respects my contributions to our lives together as living acts of commitment, I am *there* for them, with them. They're with me. This is what you do to build family links that last. I invest my time in them. Same so the other loves of my life. Because they matter. To me.

⟰ ⇩ ⟱

If you, like me, like sex and, like me, like drugs, you may like sex on drugs, like me. Or you might not. And that's cool too.

Endnotes

1. Wide-leafed Cannabis indica plants in Afghanistan and Pakistan are traditionally cultivated for the production of hashish. Pharmacologically, the wide-leafed "indica" landraces tend to have a higher cannabidiol (CBD) content than "sativa" drug strains [5]. Most commercially available "indica" strains have been selected for low levels of CBD (which is not psychoactive), with some users reporting more of a "high" and less of a "stoned" effect from "indica" compared to "sativa". Differences in the terpenoid content of the essential oil may account for some of these differences in effect[6] [7]. Common "indica" strains for recreational use are 'White Widow' and 'Northern Lights'. Source: http://en.wikipedia.org/wiki/Cannabis_indica

Questions. Answers? Order!
KathleenKBooks.com

Kathleen K. has created a library of Private Publications available at KathleenKBooks.com. Her eclectic collection features narrative fiction centered on family life in The Lent Hand (Adventures in Beach Town Towing), literate erotica (Dark Prince, Heed Thy Queen) and a case study in Post Dramatic Stress Disorder featuring Joody, a single mother allergic to responsibility.

These books are not linked by theme or genre, this is a rich collection of all-age and adults-only offerings comprising decades of production.

Becoming available for the first time in print and e-book format, these Private Publications are varied in topic but easily identifiable as Words Arranged by Kathleen K.

Info@KathleenKBooks.com